You Can Always Trust a Spotted Horse

You Can Always Trust a Spotted Horse

Stephen Bly

CROSSWAY BOOKS • WHEATON, ILLINOIS
A DIVISION OF GOOD NEWS PUBLISHERS

You Can Always Trust a Spotted Horse

Copyright © 1993 by Stephen Bly.

Published by Crossway Books, a division of Good News Publishers, 1300 Crescent St., Wheaton, Illinois 60187.

Cover illustration: David Yorke

First printing, 1992

Printed in the United States of America

ISBN 0-89107-716-2

For a list of other books by Stephen Bly or information regarding speaking engagements, write: Stephen Bly, Winchester, ID 83555.

01	00	99	98	97	96	95	94	93
15	14	13	12	11	10	9	8	7	6	5	4	3	2	1

For
ReeRee

1

*T*he piercing scream from the street made the hair on Nathan's neck bristle. A chill ran down his back as he crossed the wooden floor, boots thumping loudly. He slung the door open with a crash and banged over the sidewalk to the rail.

"Runaway!" someone hollered.

A tall black horse thundered down the street with fear in its eyes and reins tangling around its front hooves.

At least there's no rider; that horse could . . . no!

"Oh, no! He's got his spur hung up in the stirrup!" Nathan shouted as he gawked at a man on the far side of the horse being dragged on his back through the street. Nathan ran with a crowd of onlookers behind the runaway.

"Somebody's got to do something!"

"Shoot the horse!" one old man yelled.

Nathan watched a man run out in front of the stampeding mount and fire a shotgun straight into the air. The big black horse barreled over the man, knocking him to the ground.

Out of breath, Nathan came to a standstill as another man dashed out from behind the Texas Saloon. A flash of long, black hair waved under a black hat.

Tick Hill? I didn't know he was in town!

With the speed and skill of his Indian ancestors, Tick

grabbed a handful of black mane and pulled himself effortlessly aboard the stampeding horse. Nathan saw him reach down and yank the bit in his left hand, quickly circling the animal. The big black, still wide-eyed and lathering up, came to an abrupt halt.

Bystanders released the injured man and carried him off to the doctor. Several others, including Nathan, stayed with Hill and the horse.

"Tick, where did you learn to do that?"

"Riding buffalo." He dismounted and walked the horse toward the nearest rail.

"Really?" Nathan blurted.

Tick Hill turned and pulled Nathan's gray, wide-brimmed hat over his eyes.

"I rode with the Pony Express, remember? Whose horse is this?" Hill asked.

"It belongs to Williams."

"Who's Williams?"

"The fella who got drug down Main Street."

Tick Hill tied the horse to the rail and rubbed its neck. "Well, it's too hot a horse for just any rider. But it might be the fastest horse in town. How much do you reckon he'd sell it for?"

A tall man with a wide mustache replied. "Last week it would have cost you a hundred dollars . . . but at the moment, he might be in a bargainin' mood."

"If he lives, tell him I'll give him twenty dollars."

"That's a might low . . . " the other man remarked.

"It's a might high," Hill replied, "if that's all the money you have to your name."

The crowd broke up, and most headed towards the Texas Saloon. Nathan turned on his heels and clomped back towards the center of town. He had worked up a sweat chasing the horse, and his shirt felt clammy against his skin.

A shout interrupted his thoughts about fast horses. "I ain't your girlfriend, Nathan T. Riggins, and you know it!" Leah screamed above the bluster of the cold December wind.

Nathan yanked down the floppy brim of his dirty gray beaver felt hat, turned into the wind, and began to cross the street. Normally, the narrow, dirt streets of Galena, Nevada, would have been nearly impossible to navigate due to the wallow of mud, but recent freezing temperatures had stiffened the rutted road, exceeded in hardness only by the cobblestones of an eastern city.

He stood in the middle of the road and waited for a rider hiding under a muddy yellow oilcloth slicker to saunter by. After that, the Wells Station Stage lumbered past.

They've got two armed guards today . . . must be another shipment from the Shiloh.

The street finally clear, Nathan leaped up the steps of the Mercantile to where Leah stood.

In the few months that Nathan had known Leah Walker, she had alternated between liking him and hating him, changing at least as often as reports of new gold strikes hit town. Three months before he was a good four inches taller than Leah, but now she had caught up with him. She had pulled her knit cap down over her ears. Her brown bangs shot out over her eyebrows, and her long hair was brushed back behind her head.

"Why do you have to yell across the street?" Nathan asked. "Couldn't you just walk over there and talk to me?"

"You ain't my boyfriend, that's why," she repeated. "And don't go around telling folks you is!"

"When did I ever say I was your boyfriend?"

"Katie McGregor told me that she heard you tell a man at the bank that you was my boyfriend. Well, you ain't."

Nathan frowned and looked Leah straight in the eyes. "Are you wearing perfume?" he suddenly asked.

"I ain't got no perfume . . . I been eatin' a peppermint. But don't you go changin' the subject."

"Some man dressed in a black topcoat said, 'Son, do you know where the Walker family lives?' and I said, 'Yes. Leah Walker is a very good friend of mine.'"

"I ain't your girlfriend."

"I know that!" Nathan chimed in. "But you are my friend, aren't you?"

"Yeah . . . but it ain't one bit romantic or nothin' like that, and don't you forget it."

Romantic? Where does she get that? Sometimes it's like Leah and me are in a school play, but we're reading parts off different scripts.

Nathan changed the subject. "Leah, have you seen Colin?"

"He's gone. Went with his mama to Wells Station on the stage."

"He what? He was supposed to go with me out to old Skeeter's cabin! You would think he would tell me if he was leaving town."

"What ya going out to Skeeter's for?"

"To look at a horse."

"You still ain't bought yourself a horse?"

"No one wants to sell anything except old swaybacks."

"I'll go with you out to Skeeter's," she offered.

"Nah . . . it wouldn't look right," he teased. "After all, you aren't my girlfriend."

"I know I ain't your girlfriend, but I'm a good friend. You

said so yourself!" she huffed. She flipped her head back trying to get the bangs out of her eyes.

"Okay," he said nodding, "you can go, but you have to promise me there won't be any of that romantic stuff."

Leah slugged him in the arm.

Nathan jumped back, and his boot caught a nail head in the wooden sidewalk. He tripped and sprawled across a bench in front of the store.

Suddenly Nathan's dog dashed out from between the buildings and growled menacingly at Leah.

"Tona! Don't you bare your teeth at me, you worthless coyote!" Leah bossed. Then she turned back to Nathan, "Are you going to let me go with you or not?"

"Can you get a horse to ride?"

"My daddy's gone to Austin, and *she* won't let me ride hers." Leah scurried along the wooden sidewalk, trying to keep up with Nathan who took long strides towards the marshal's office.

"She? Why don't you call her Mary? Or Mrs. Walker? Or Mother, or—"

"She ain't my mother! You know she ain't my mother!"

Nathan started to say something, but seeing Leah's brown eyes glaring at him, he reconsidered.

"Go get your heaviest coat and meet me at the corrals," he instructed. "I'll see which horses Dad will let me have. Tell Mary, eh . . . Mrs. Walker . . . that you'll be gone a couple hours."

"She don't care about nothin' as long as I don't get the floor dirty and do eat all my supper."

Leah ran off in the opposite direction as Nathan opened the door to his father's office. The brass door handle was icy cold.

∎

Jugs wasn't Nathan's idea of a great horse. He had one speed—slow, and only one place he wanted to go—home.

That's why Dad always gives me Jugs. I won't fall off, and he'll get me home. When I get my horse, it will be the quickest horse in northern Nevada! I'll call him Chinook because he'll blow by so fast that it'll catch them all by surprise. He'll be tall and black with a high head and a flowing mane. Sort of like that runaway, but better mannered. And I'll get Mr. Rodriguez to make me a silver bit and—

"Where's my horse?"

Nathan jerked around to see Leah with an old wool blanket wrapped around her shoulders.

"Is that your coat?" he asked.

"Is that our only horse?" she whined.

"Eh . . . yeah, Dad said we could double up on Jugs."

Leah curled her lip and wrinkled her nose. "Oh, that's just great."

Nathan jerked the cinch tight and adjusted the stirrup. The leather was stiff and hard to work.

"Look, if you don't want to go—"

"I'm goin'!" Leah insisted. She watched Nathan climb into the saddle. Then she held out her right arm, and he yanked her up behind him. Nathan pulled his hat low, tightened up the stampede string, and buttoned the top button of his heavy jacket.

"You want some of this blanket?" Leah asked.

"No, I don't need a blanket!" he growled.

"Is Tona coming with us?"

The dog lay low beside the corral gate.

"Tona goes wherever he wants to. I suppose he will trot along for a while."

■

Green trees are sparse in northern Nevada in the summertime. And in December, there isn't a green tree for five hundred miles. Just steel gray sage, shivering in the wind and granite outcroppings jutting from snow-sprinkled mountains, flanked by smooth tailing piles left by the hordes of summer prospectors.

Nathan rode straight east of town to the frozen creek and then turned Jugs north. Leah bounced behind him, lacing the leather cantle strings around her left wrist and clutching the blanket at her neck with her right.

"What kind of horse does Skeeter have for sale?" she asked.

"Mr. Melton said Skeeter would sell Spider for fifty cash dollars."

"Ain't that the black horse that won the race on the Fourth of July?"

"Yep."

Leah pulled herself closer to the back of the saddle. "You going to buy him with the reward money we got from turning in Lexie Devere?"

"Yeah . . . if Spider's sound," Nathan reported. "I'm not buying any lame horse."

"How can you tell if he's sound?" she asked.

"I can just tell, that's how!" he snapped. "Did you hear about Devere?"

"Did he bust out of jail again?" She sat up and let the blanket slip low on her shoulders.

"He tried."

"They caught him?"

"Shot him dead."

"Devere's dead?" she gasped.

"Yep."

"Says who?"

"I read the report from Carson City in my dad's office."

Leah remained silent for several minutes.

"Nathan," she finally said, "I'm glad he's dead."

"Why?"

"'Cause I was afraid he'd get out and come back and hurt us."

Nathan kicked his spurs into Jugs as they rode up a steep draw, but the horse ignored the command. Leah's strong hands grabbed his waist until they made it to the top of the climb.

"Nate, is it wrong for me to be glad that Devere's dead? Do you think God will be mad at me for thinkin' that?"

"Well . . . " Nathan paused to try to think of a response. "I guess we have to be honest . . . anyway, I'm glad to know we won't have to look up and see him holding a gun on us again."

"Nathan, did you bring a gun?"

"Just my carbine. Why?"

"Nothin'."

After a few silent minutes, she spoke again. "What happens to people when they die?"

"They go to Heaven or . . . you know, that other place," Nathan muttered.

"Where do you think Devere is?" she pressed.

"That's up to Jesus." Nathan waved his hand towards a clump of leafless cottonwoods. "Look, there's Skeeter's cabin!"

"He must be at home. There's smoke in the chimney," she reported. The curling wood smoke hung low to the ground, and Nathan could smell its bitter aroma as they approached.

"I don't see Spider."

"There's a horse over there in the corral," she said pointing.

"Some short rat-tail standing in the snow. That's not my idea of a sound horse."

"Is that Skeeter?" she asked.

"Where?"

"On the porch, holding that rifle."

"Ho! On the porch!" Nathan called. "Can we ride up?"

The man pushed his hat back, revealing dark hair and a wide smile. "It will be a pleasure to have some company," he shouted. "Is that your dog?"

Nathan glanced back at Tona slinking in the distance. "Yeah." Then they rode closer to the porch but remained mounted.

"I'm Nathan T. Riggins from Galena and this is Leah."

"And I'm Temple Cholach, but most folks call me Temp." The tall, muscular man glanced at Nathan and then at Leah. "Say, you two ain't married, are ya?" He laughed.

"I ain't even his girlfriend!" Leah fumed.

"Where's Skeeter?" Nathan asked. "I heard he had a horse for sale."

"Skeeter packed on out of here two days ago. Said he was going up to the Owyhees. Silver City, I suppose. I'm just ridin' line camps lookin' for winter work. Skeeter said I could bunk here as long as I wanted."

The man propped his rifle against the front door and stepped out to Nathan and Leah. Nathan could see his broad shoulders and tanned face. He brushed back his thick black mustache, and Nathan noticed deep creases around his eyes.

"You two out horse buying, are you?"

"Just looking, mainly," Nathan responded, not wanting to reveal whether he had money on him.

"Well, let me give you some advice. Find yourself a spotted horse like ol' Onepenny out there."

"Spotted horse?" Leah asked.

"That ain't snow on his rump, you know. That's his markin's. A snow blanket on the rump, white in the eyes, stripes on the hoofs, wispy tail and scant mane—he's a Palouse horse, and a good one. Smartest, toughest, hard-workin' mount I ever owned. I bought him from some Nez Perce up in the Wallowas."

"Kind of small, isn't he?" Nathan asked.

"Stands 14.5, but it's not the size that matters. Why don't you two just sit on the porch and let me show you what good horseflesh looks like."

Cholach stepped out to the brush corral and swung open the sagging gate. Without even a signal, the horse trotted to the man and trailed along behind him as he walked over to the cabin. Onepenny ignored the occasional yap by Tona and stood still as Cholach tossed on a blanket and set the saddle down lightly.

"Did you ever saddle up that horse of yours without a lead rope tied to a rail?" he asked.

"No, sir," Nathan replied.

"Don't you got no bridle? No bit? No reins?" Leah questioned.

"Sure, I got 'em . . . but I don't need them."

Grabbing the horn with his left hand, he swung up onto the saddle.

"How you going to control him without reins?" Nathan shouted.

"Watch!"

Nathan sensed immediately he was looking at a very good horse and a great horse-trainer.

Temple Cholach rode the horse around the yard in a figure eight pattern while keeping his arms folded against his chest.

"How does the horse know what to do?" Leah asked.

"Leg commands," Cholach instructed.

He backed the horse up, and he had it walk sideways. He stood up in the saddle and rode around the yard again. Then he had Onepenny bow to Leah while he remained on its back.

Cholach rode over to the rail in front of the cabin and climbed off the horse. Standing on the rail and leaning against the eave of the house, he clapped his hands twice. Onepenny trotted about fifty feet up the trail away from the cabin. The gelding stopped and turned back to Cholach.

"What's he doing?" Nathan quizzed.

"Waiting for my command." Then Cholach let fly with a short high whistle, and Onepenny cantered up to the hitching post. The cowboy leaped to the horse's back without missing a stride. They circled the yard and galloped straight at the corral fence that stood a good five feet high. Nathan's mouth dropped open when rider and bridleless horse jumped the fence and circled the inside of the corral.

Cholach dismounted and walked out of the corral, striding towards the cabin.

"You forgot to shut the gate, Mister!" Leah yelled.

"He'll stay." Cholach motioned with a flip of the hand.

"You . . . eh . . . wouldn't be wanting to sell Onepenny, would you?" Nathan haltingly asked.

"What? I thought you said you weren't interested in that little rat-tail."

"I've changed my mind," Nathan admitted.

"Well . . . one of these days I just might up and sell him. How much you willing to pay?"

"He's got fifty cash dollars!" Leah blurted out.

"Leah!" Nathan shouted in disgust.

"I mean, in the bank in Galena," she added.

"He's probably worth more than that," Nathan mumbled.

"You're right . . . but who knows. The day might come when I need that fifty. You want to ride him?"

"Me?" Nathan squeaked in a high-pitched voice.

"Sure, I'll let you cheat and have a headstall, bit, and reins."

For the next thirty minutes, Nathan rode the smoothest horse he had ever mounted. Even though Onepenny's rump was wide, his withers were narrow, and Nathan didn't feel like he was being split in two. The slightest command with the reins brought instant response.

"Nathan, I'm cold. Maybe we ought to go back to town," Leah called.

Reluctantly he dismounted and handed the reins to Temp Cholach. Only then did Nathan notice that his fingers were just about numb.

"You can come out and ride him anytime, son."

"Honest?"

"Until I drift on out of here."

"Thank you, sir. I'll do that."

"Temple . . . just call me Temple."

The cool winter sun was just an orange ball resting on distant purple mountains when Nathan turned back to Galena. It was a spectacular sight—one of those bright western vistas that people back East can't even imagine.

But Nathan missed seeing it.

He was lost in a daydream about a spotted horse.

2

*L*ook at this! It's a complete waste of telegraph time—that's what it is!" Marshal Riggins jammed his hat on a hook by the kitchen door and flopped down next to Nathan and his mother at the supper table.

"Bad news, Dad?" Nathan asked.

"It's no news. Look at this, Nate."

With the official dispatch clutched in both hands, Nathan held it up to the light.

His father continued, "Sheriff Hannagan up in Idaho telegraphed to say that some stagecoach robber had made off with a haul and was headed this way. Only thing is, he didn't have the man's name or description; nor did he know what kind of horse he was riding."

"Well," Nathan's mom chided, "that narrows it down to every man in Nevada."

"Exactly my point. It could be anyone from John Doe to Colt Blueman!"

"Did I tell you about the horse I saw—"

"Nathan, don't interrupt your father."

" . . . why send a telegram that tells you absolutely nothing? They treat the wire like it was a toy. It has no more meaning than the conversation of two old men out in front of the Miners' Hall." He spun his head towards Nathan. "What horse? That breakaway?"

"That's a really fast horse. Did I tell you how Tick Hill jumped it? Man, I've never seen anything—"

"I saw Williams over at Doc Gooding's. He's got a broken foot, ripped-up back, and a headache that will last until the next century. He said you couldn't pay him to climb aboard that broncho again."

Nathan scooped some potatoes onto his plate and cleared his throat. "Tick offered to buy the horse for twenty dollars."

"And Williams said he wouldn't sell it for less than fifty."

For a moment Nathan stared at his buttermilk biscuit trying to decide whether to cover it with cherry preserves or honey.

"Dad, do you think that black is the fastest horse in Galena?"

"Probably the fastest in Lander County . . . providing someone could stay on it. A fast horse that you can't ride is nothin' but a hay-burnin' aggravation. Are you thinking about buying it?" he asked.

Nathan sat up and scratched the back of his head.

"No. I mean . . . I was considering it for a while this afternoon."

"Give yourself about four more years. Then you'll be big enough for a horse like that," his dad advised. "But I'll say this—it's a fine-looking horse."

"Actually," Nathan stammered, "I . . . eh . . . found another horse that I like even better."

"Did you go out to see Skeeter?" his mother asked.

"Yes and no. I mean, I did go out to Skeeter's, but he was gone up to Silver City. Leah and me—"

"Leah went with you?"

"Yeah, Colin's out of town, and Leah wanted to go. Dad said it was okay."

"David?" Nathan's mother lifted her eyebrows at his father as she spoke.

"They're just twelve, Adele," he justified himself.

"And how old were you when you showed up at Daddy's back door trying to sell that sickly old hog?" she teased.

A quick rap at the door ended the conversation. A deep voice called out, "Marshal? There's a drunk miner over at the Cherokee who refuses to pay his tab. He's waving a revolver around like a flag on the Fourth of July. Can you or Deputy Haley come settle him down?"

Mr. Riggins grabbed his hat and his Winchester and went out the door.

"Mom, I did find a great horse. He's a Palouse horse, you know—"

"Nate, I don't know much about horses . . . but I do know there's not enough wood in here to last until morning. You split a couple arm loads and fill the wood box before it gets dark. You can talk horses when your father gets home."

Nathan crammed the last bites down, pulled on his coat, and trudged out behind the house.

I didn't even get to tell them about Onepenny! They don't think I know how to pick a horse. That would be something . . . I just come riding in here on that spotted horse, back it up to the door, circle around the yard, jump over the woodpile. I wonder if Mr. Cholach will teach me how to jump the horse? He said maybe he'd sell me the horse someday . . . maybe I should earn more money. I'll just surprise Dad. That's what I'll do. "Oh, this horse?" I'll say. "Why, I bought him off some Indians up in the Wallowas." Nah, I'll tell him the truth, but he will be amazed!

Nathan continued a running dialog with himself as he set wood rounds on the stump and swung the six-pound axe, scattering pine in every direction. The pine logs were splitting easily, and Nathan enjoyed the steady strain on his arm and shoulder muscles. Even though it was cold enough for his breath to fog, he had sweated through his wool shirt when he was finished.

Loading up the wood box, he hung his coat on a hook and pulled a chair up to the table where his mother was kneading bread dough for breakfast.

"Did you finish your Bible reading today?" she queried.

"Yep."

"And your grammar? Did you compete the assignment?"

Nathan pulled a brown tattered volume from an apple crate next to the table.

"Sure. Remember, I showed it to you this morning?"

His mother brushed her hair back out of her face, and Nathan noticed the creases around her eyes. "Well, just because Miss D'Imperio is in St. Louis for the holidays is no excuse to get behind on your lessons."

"No, ma'am," he said nodding. "I was just going to read some more in my book."

"Washington Irving?"

"Yeah." Nathan formally pronounced, "*The ADVENTURES of Captain Bonneville, U.S.A., in the ROCKY MOUNTAINS and the FAR WEST.*"

"Well, where are you in the story?"

"At the gathering in Green River. Is that in Utah or up in Wyoming?" he asked.

"I'm afraid I just don't know. That's a question for your father."

"I've got a question for you." Nathan paused and then continued, "How come Leah runs around all over town telling everyone that she's not my girlfriend?"

"She does?"

"Yep."

"Is she your girlfriend?"

"Of course not," Nathan insisted.

"But you did go horseback riding with her all afternoon."

"Sure, but that don't make her my girlfriend."

"Doesn't."

"Doesn't," Nathan repeated. "Does it?"

"Perhaps not now. But next year you do the same thing, and everyone will think she's your girlfriend. Leah will be a young lady then."

"In one year?" Nathan inquired. "How does that work?"

"That's another question for your father," his mother mumbled. "Listen, after you read a few pages, hike on over to your father's office and see if he knows when he will be home. We'll wait up for him if he's not going to be too late."

Nathan was still trying to figure out the value of Bonneville's twenty-two and a half packs of beaver pelts, weighing one hundred pounds each, at $3.50 per pound in St. Louis, when his mother reminded him to check on his father.

"Come straight home if he's not at the office," she instructed. "It's just too cold to wander up and down the streets looking for him."

"Mom?" Nathan jammed on his hat. "I'm going to find myself a really good horse."

"Have you prayed about it?"

"What? I mean . . . the Lord doesn't want to be bothered with things like that, does He?"

"Why don't you take time and ask Him?"

"Yeah . . . I think I will."

As Nathan left the house, he pulled his hat low and buttoned his coat all the way down. Halfway across the street, he felt his face stiffen in the cold, and his canvas ducking trousers chafed his legs. He knew his ears would be throbbing before he got home. His boots crunched across the frozen dirt roadway.

The kerosene lanterns cast peculiar shadows out the windows and across the street. There was absolutely no wind. No stars littered the sky, and he guessed that heavy, dark clouds hung just beyond the borders of his vision.

It's going to snow tonight. If it blows all night, they won't let me go out to Skeeter's cabin. If it gets too cold, Mr. Cholach could ride on out. Lord, listen, it's me—Nathan. I sure would like to buy that horse, Onepenny. Now I know You're busy with important problems . . . but, well, I would like Your help. Thanks.

"Young Riggins! Is that you?"

The urgency in the voice shot through Nathan's thoughts and chilled his bones.

"Who's th-there?" he stammered into the darkness.

"Tick Hill. Listen, run get your mama. Your daddy's been shot, up at the Cherokee!"

"Shot!" Nathan shouted. "How bad?"

"I don't know . . . I'm goin' to get Doc Gooding!" Hill's voice faded with the sound of retreating footsteps.

"Lord! Forget about the horse. I don't need a horse, God. I need a dad . . . please, Lord . . . please!"

Twice he stumbled and fell to the cold, hard roadway.

Twice he sprang back to his feet and continued to stagger through the dark. Tears streamed down his face. He didn't bother to wipe them away.

"Mother!" he cried out from the front door. "Daddy's been shot! He's down at the Cherokee!"

Nathan expected his mother to burst into tears.

Or faint.

Or run out the door to the Cherokee.

He was wrong on all three counts.

Instead, she carefully placed the bread dough in a crock and began to wash the flour off her hands.

"Nathan, get my heavy coat out of the bedroom. Who told you he was shot?"

"Tick Hill . . . he was running to get the doc."

She glanced in a little mirror above the table by the door and quickly ran a comb through her hair.

"Shouldn't we hurry?" Nathan insisted.

"Bring the small lantern," she ordered. "I'll get your father a fresh shirt and trousers."

"A shirt? What if . . . what if he's . . . you know!"

"Dead?"

"Yeah."

"Then all our hurrying won't make any difference."

Within moments they were walking up the sidewalk. The Cherokee was on the far side of town, six blocks away. Nathan wanted desperately to run, but he was carrying the lantern and lagged back to provide light for his mother.

"I don't understand, Mom. You don't seem very upset."

"Nathan, don't let looks deceive you. I'm dying a thousand deaths on the inside. I can't imagine life going on without your father. But he made me promise him three things when he took this marshal's job. I am not to panic every time I hear he's been shot. I am to conduct myself with dignity in the event that he really is shot. And I'm to bring him fresh clothing."

"Dad told you all that?"

"Yes, he did. He also told me that he would more likely be shot sometime by a drunk who just wanted to hurrah the town than by a professional shootist."

"Mother, are you really scared?"

"Yes, I am really scared."

"Did you pray?"

"Yes, I did . . . did you?"

25

"Yes, ma'am."

"Well, I guess we'll have to trust the Lord on this one."

Nathan had never stepped inside the Cherokee, but this time he didn't hesitate to follow his mother through the swinging doors. Both tobacco smoke and gun smoke hung in the air. Most of the men had scattered to the far wall or the bar.

Nathan saw one man whom he didn't know lying motionless on the floor. Several men stooped on the other side of a table, and Nathan spotted his father sitting on the floor with his back against a chair. Doctor Gooding was wrapping his shoulder with a white cloth.

"David?" his mother's shaky voice called.

"Adele!" His father looked up, shook his head, and then tried to smile. "What's a beautiful lady like you doing in a crummy place like the Cherokee?"

"I just came to take my husband home. I warned him for years about hanging around this side of town."

"Did you bring a clean shirt?"

"Yes . . . do you want it now?"

"Yep. I wouldn't want to look sloppy on the job."

"I also brought your son." She nodded towards Nathan.

Nathan's tears flowed across his face and dripped onto his coat. "Dad . . . are you . . . are you going to be . . . I mean, is it serious?"

"I'll be sore and stiff for a couple of months," Mr. Riggins admitted. "But I should be back in the saddle in a day or so."

"Did you kill him?" Nathan pointed to the other man on the floor.

"I'm afraid so. He started aiming the gun at folks, and when I went to disarm him, he shot me."

"So you had to protect yourself?"

"Yeah . . . but he was drunk. A man does stupid things

when drunk—things he would never in a thousand years try when sober."

"Who is he, Dad?"

"I don't even know his name. Help me up, son."

Nathan couldn't remember when his father had ever needed his help before. Leaning on Nathan's shoulder, and with assistance from his wife, Marshal Riggins pulled on the clean plaid shirt.

"Haley?" The marshal spoke to his deputy. "You take charge here. See if you can find anything out about this man. We'll need to notify his family. Adele, maybe you could assist me on the left side?"

"You'll need some help," Haley insisted.

"Nope . . . we'll just take her slow," the marshal responded.

For the next few moments, father, mother, and son slowly worked their way down the darkened sidewalk.

"I don't know why he had to shoot me," his dad said softly. "I had to shoot back."

"You were just doing your job," Mrs. Riggins comforted him.

Marshal Riggins stopped to catch his breath. "Well, whiskey won another round tonight."

They spoke very little after that. When they got to the house, Mrs. Riggins had Nathan take his father straight to bed.

Stoking the fire, Nathan waited for his mother to come out of the bedroom. Carrying a lantern, she finally walked slowly back to Nathan.

"Is he going to be, you know, okay?"

"Yes, I believe so. The bullet went through, and the doctor was able to stop the bleeding. He's sleeping now . . . just as long as he doesn't get infected . . ."

Suddenly his mother's voice diminished, and Nathan

watched her flop down on a bench by the table. She folded her arms on the table and laid her head down on her arms. Then she began to sob.

Nathan felt helpless.

He didn't know what to say.

His mother continued to cry.

Finally, he scurried over to her. "He's going to be okay, Mother. It's just a shoulder wound. The doctor will take care of him. It's okay, Mama . . . it's okay!"

"I know. I know, Nate. I was . . . I was just so scared . . . I can't let your father hear me cry. Don't tell him I'm such a baby. Don't tell him, Nathan."

"No, ma'am. I won't tell him," he promised.

Finally, Nathan fixed his mother a cup of tea from the kettle on the stove. He put the cup by her side. Then he turned off all the lanterns except the one on the kitchen table.

"Mama, I'm going to bed now. Are you all right?"

He didn't wake her up for a reply.

■

Nathan woke up in the middle of the night when he thought he heard his mother crying. But he went back to sleep and slept soundly the rest of the night. It was the smell of salt pork sizzling that woke him the next morning. He didn't dress, but staggered out to the table wearing his flannel nightshirt.

"Dad? Wh-what are you doing up?" he stammered.

"I'm going to have a little meat and eggs and biscuits, I hope. Get yourself dressed, and bring in some wood for your mother."

"Yes, sir." Nathan turned toward his room, but then he

whipped back around. "Dad . . . are you, you know . . . all right?"

"Well, my right arm and shoulder feel like they're going to burn off or fall off, and my headache's something fierce. But I can pull through that. It takes more than this to stop a Riggins, doesn't it? Now, go on."

"Yes, sir."

Nathan slipped on his clothes and boots and grabbed his heavy coat. Then he clomped towards the back door and met his mom in the pantry. She was wearing her nicest Sunday dress, her hair carefully combed back and a big smile on her face.

"You sure look pretty, Mom!" he blurted out.

"Why, thank you," she replied in a teasing voice. "You're the second handsome gentleman to tell me that this morning."

"Are you feeling better?" he whispered.

"Yes . . . and thanks for keeping my secret."

■

To Nathan's amazement, his predicted snowstorm the previous night had disappeared. A warming breeze blew, and the streets began to thaw into muddy barriers.

Shortly after breakfast Leah Walker called Nathan out to the street.

"Is your daddy . . . d-d-dead?" she stuttered.

"Nope. Just shoulder shot."

"He killed a man last night, didn't he?"

"Yep."

"Was you scared?"

"Yep."

"Did you cry?"

"Yep."

"Is he going to quit marshalin'?"

"Nope."

"Did you tell them about Onepenny?"

"Nope."

"Are you going to let me go out with you and visit that spotted horse today?"

"Nope."

"Nope? Yep? Is that all you're going to say to me?"

"Yep."

"Nathan T. Riggins," Leah fumed, "just 'cause I ain't your girlfriend ain't no reason to treat me poorly! And I definitely ain't your girlfriend!"

"Leah, if you tell me that one more time," Nathan raved, "I'm—I'm—I'm going to believe it!"

"Well, you'd better . . . " Her voice trailed off into silence.

3

*N*athan talked Captain McSwain at the Galena Livery & Feed into letting him take a tall white mare out to Skeeter's place. The Chinook wind had turned the road into a bog by noon. He wanted to race out to the cabin, but he knew the mare would chuck mud from head to toe if she ever started to trot.

Even though he couldn't imagine needing it, he tied his jacket to the back of his cantle and plodded out of town. About halfway to Skeeter's cabin, Nathan spotted the Shiloh Mine coach rattling toward him. He scooted the mare off the road and down a side trail to let the wagon pass.

They're throwing so much mud off those wheels that the drag riders have to ride point with the others. Now this road will freeze all rutted up. It won't be decent to ride on until spring.

The trail from the wagon road up to Skeeter's was on the north side of a long slope and had not thawed out as fast. Nathan picked up the pace but then drew to an abrupt stop when he heard gunfire coming from the direction of the cabin.

He glanced down at his carbine, still buttoned tight in his scabbard. Nathan's first reaction was to turn around and go home.

But he didn't.

Maybe Mr. Cholach is hunting . . . but there's a lot of shots . . . still, the shots are measured . . . aren't they?

Nathan rode the mare up over the draw so he could view the cabin, which stood about a half mile away. The hue of the building blended into the mountain, and only the blue sky and bright afternoon sun added any color to the scene.

Searching the horizon for activity, Nathan sighted the spotted horse in the brush corral and no other animals. The shots continued and sounded as if they were coming from the cabin itself. Nathan approached slowly, straining to see some activity.

As he closed in on the leafless cottonwoods near the corral, he finally saw Temple Cholach on the back side of the cabin. He was setting punctured tins on a rotting log. He waved Nathan in and then took three more shots, each time sailing the airtights high in the air.

"Nathan, I'm just keeping in practice. Come on, grab your revolver, and you can practice with me."

"I don't have a handgun. My daddy says I don't need one."

"Well, now, that's very true." Cholach holstered his gun, picked up his coat that had been draped over a half-broken fence post, and walked toward Nathan.

"You had any dinner? I'm going to scrape up some beans, and you're welcome to join me."

"Yes, sir, I already ate my dinner—about noon."

"Sir? Now you listen, you call me Temple or Temp . . . but not sir."

Nathan slid off the mare and tied her to the rail nearest the cabin. His legs felt stiff at the joints. "Mr. Cholach . . . I mean, Temp. I been thinking a lot since yesterday about that spotted horse."

"Onepenny?"

"Yeah. Let's just say you decided, you know, someday to sell him. How much would you ask for him?"

Cholach walked slowly to the corral. "You want him pretty bad, don't you?"

"Yes, sir . . . I mean, Temp. It's just exactly the kind of horse I've spent the last couple of months looking for."

"Well, Nate, I don't always buy and sell horses. Sometimes I just trade in goods. You know—a saddle, a steer, another horse—things like that."

"What would you trade him for?" Nathan pressed.

"Let me ponder that a spell. I'll grab some chuck, and you exercise Onepenny for me."

"You mean ride him?"

"Yep."

Nathan spent little time transferring his saddle from the mare to the spotted horse. Within moments he was on horseback, trotting down the mountain to the creek and then galloping back to the corral. He had just finished backing Onepenny completely around the cabin and considered trying to stand up on the saddle when Temple Cholach rejoined him.

"Ol' Onepenny loves to do his tricks, don't he?" Cholach called out.

"Yeah," Nathan responded. "Could I . . . eh, you know, jump him?"

"You ever jumped a horse?"

"Only over creeks and logs."

"Well, give it a try. Just remember to hit him with your spurs right at the last moment, then lean forward, hold on tight, and put all your weight on your knees."

Nathan circled Onepenny around the yard and then kicked his spurs into the gelding. The spotted horse flew towards the corral fence. Just as they closed in on it, Nathan kicked again, stood in the stirrups, and tucked his head behind Onepenny's ears.

The spotted horse flew over the fence, landing with a hard thud. Nathan slammed down into the saddle, but he held on.

"I did it!" he shouted. "It wasn't very pretty, but I did it!"

"Well, you sure do look like a natural on him. Maybe I should . . ."

"Sell him? Are you going to sell him to me?" Nathan shouted.

"You ain't heard my terms yet."

"No, sir, I . . . I mean, Temp. No, I haven't."

"Well, I wouldn't make this deal to another living soul, but I'll consider trading him to you for the fastest, dark-colored, long-legged horse you can find and a fancy silver necklace."

"You will? You mean it? Onepenny's mine?"

"Nope. Not until you bring the goods. I've got to pull out for Idaho by noon tomorrow. Think I'll take advantage of this mild weather."

"Noon tomorrow?"

"Yep. Can you do it?"

"I know just the horse. It's black and my daddy says it's the fastest horse in Nevada—at least in Lander County, that is."

"Sounds like what I need. I can make a little spending money around the cow camps if I can outrace some of the boys. It could get me by until spring. Can you have him here at noon?"

"I think so."

"And the necklace?"

"Silver, right?" Nathan countered.

"Oh, something real pretty . . . it's for a young lady who's mighty sweet on me, if you get the drift. I always try to bring her a present."

"I've never bought one, but I'll do my best."

"Nate, let me be real honest. I just got to pack on out of here by noon. So if you ain't made it, or you can't find a necklace and a fast horse, well . . . I'll just have to leave anyway, you understand? It ain't nothin' personal."

"I'll be here."

"Can you get that black horse?"

"Yep. Mr. Williams wants to sell it in the worst way. Eh . . . Temp? Listen, that black horse is pretty hot-blooded and kind of hard to ride. I didn't want to trick you into thinking it was a proper horse."

"Nate, if it's a fast horse, then it's got to be jumpy. Don't worry about me. I'll be able to cover the saddle on it. But will you be able to get him here?"

"Oh, I'll get him here if I have to lead him the whole way."

Nathan spent several minutes brushing down the spotted horse. He opened Onepenny's mouth and glanced at the teeth. Then he circled the pony, picked up and carefully examined each hoof.

Shoes are tight . . . frogs look healthy. Lord . . . I really, really want this horse!

While Temple Cholach split firewood, Nathan spent a good half hour sitting on the corral gate staring at Onepenny. Finally, he noticed his rear end getting sore. He jumped down and walked over to Cholach.

"Eh . . . Temp? Is Onepenny always this calm?"

"Yep. You can rope off him, work cattle with him, or leave him tied to the rail on a Saturday night. He sure doesn't spook easy. You can shoot squirrels from the saddle, I can tell you that. Say, I think that Chinook's let up. The temperature will be dropping as soon as the sun goes down."

"Yeah, I'd better go back to town. I have a black horse to buy."

"I'll see you tomorrow."

"Yes, sir. I'll be here."

"Give my regards to your girlfriend," Cholach teased.

"She isn't my . . . " Nathan noticed the man's wide smile.

"Yeah. I'll tell Leah you mentioned her." Nathan cinched up the white mare and led her out to the yard.

Within minutes he rode down the mountain slope, out of sight of the cabin. Somewhere before he reached Galena, the temperature dropped a good twenty degrees, and he pulled on his coat.

The next time I ride home from Skeeter's cabin, I'll be mounted on Onepenny—my Onepenny!

■

Sometimes the Chinook winds thaw out northern Nevada for several days. This time it was only a few hours. By the time Nathan reached Galena, the roadway was beginning to freeze again.

His first stop was home—to discover that his dad was asleep, and his mother had left a note saying she was at the meat market.

He was running down the sidewalk when Leah stopped him. "Nathan! Guess what I decided?" she shouted as she sprinted to catch up with him.

"You're going to be nice to your stepmother?" he suggested.

She put her hands on her hips and frowned.

"No! I've decided that it would be all right if you wanted me to be your girlfriend after all."

"You what?"

"I ain't goin' to marry you, of course. But that's no reason I couldn't be your girlfriend for a while."

"Leah, listen . . . I don't think . . . look, I've got to go buy a horse. We'll talk about this later."

"'We'll talk about it later'? Is that all you're goin' to say? You treat me like we was married. I reckon we won't talk about it later! I take it all back, so there!"

Lord, I don't think I can keep up with her changin' her mind!

Nathan ran on down the sidewalk to the Starbuck Hotel. Still panting, he asked the short, bald clerk behind the counter, "Which room is Mr. Williams in?"

"Number 6," the man replied. "But he's been in bed most all day. Don't disturb him unless it's an emergency."

"This is an emergency!" Nathan vaulted the stairs two at a time.

Banging on the door, he called out, "Mr. Williams? Sorry to disturb your rest. I need to talk to you about buying that black horse."

"Come in . . . come in!" a voice shouted.

Nathan pushed the door open to an aroma of tobacco smoke, stale food, and dirty clothes. The floor of the room was strewn with bottles, newspapers, discarded clothing, and half-eaten plates of food. Wrapped in a green wool blanket on the middle of a sheetless mattress was Mr. Williams.

"Fifty dollars. Won't consider selling him for a penny less."

"Mr. Williams, I'll be straight out with you. I'll give you forty for the black horse."

"Fifty."

"Forty, and I'll clean your room for you."

"Forty-five, and you clean the room."

Nathan shook his head. "Nope. No cleaning the room for forty-five."

"Forty-two fifty?" Williams bartered.

"And clean the room?"

"Just haul out the trash and bring me a plate of supper."

"Do I have to pay for the supper?"

"Yep."

"It's a deal!" Nathan ran to the bed and shook the man's hand.

"Now that you're a horse owner," the man swung his legs over to the edge of the mattress and sat up, "just what are you going to do with that horse? He's too hot to ride."

"I can ride him," Nathan boasted.

"Does your daddy know you're buyin' that horse?"

"Look, do you want my cash money or not?" Nathan insisted.

"Your silver and gold is as good as anyone's. You go grab me some supper, and I'll write out a bill of sale."

Nathan scurried down the stairs of the Starbuck and into the Wild Horse Cafe next door. Within minutes he was carrying a bulging tin plate of meat and potatoes in one hand and a cup of steaming coffee in the other. He worked his way up to Room 6, stepping lightly, careful not to spill anything.

Mr. Williams watched from his sitting position on the bed as Nathan picked up the room and packed the trash out back to the burn barrel. Within moments, he banged his way back into the man's room.

"You got the bill of sale?"

"You got the money?"

"Forty-two fifty."

"Forty-five," the man insisted.

"You said forty-two fifty!" Nathan groaned.

"Oh . . . did I? Well, here's the paper."

Nathan counted out the exact amount in silver and gold coins. They were heavy, but warm from being crammed in his pocket. Then he took the paper.

"Thank you, Mr. Williams."

"Sure . . . listen, son, don't get yourself hurt on that mount. He can be mighty mean."

"Yes, sir, I'll be careful."

Nathan folded the bill of sale and slipped it into his coat pocket and once again sprinted out of the Starbuck.

"Tona!" Nathan shouted as his thin gray and white dog joined him in front of the hotel, "I own a horse! A very fast horse! But not the right horse . . . yet!" He turned down the alley to cut over to the stables.

It was almost sundown when Nathan finished checking on his new horse. He started home, then stopped abruptly.

The necklace!

He turned towards the Galena Mercantile and shoved the tall, narrow door open. A wave of heat radiating from the wood stove in the middle of the room rolled over him. Unbuttoning his jacket and pushing back his gray hat, Nathan raced over to a clerk.

"Hey, Nate, we're about to close for the night. What can I get you?"

"I want a silver necklace."

"A necklace! You mean—for your mother?"

"No, Jared, it's for a girlfriend."

"Your girlfriend?"

"No . . . it's this friend of mine. He has a girlfriend."

"And he wants you to buy a necklace for him to give to his girl? Sure, whatever you say." The clerk winked at Nathan.

"Here's what I got—some mighty fine silver plate for only seventy-five cents."

"I want real silver," Nathan demanded.

"That'll cost you good money."

"I've got five dollars."

"This is a serious girlfriend . . . now it wouldn't be for that cute little Leah, would it?"

Nathan pulled his hat down low on his forehead. "I told you it's for a friend!"

"Well, I don't have any five-dollar necklaces," the clerk admitted.

"I've got to buy a necklace!"

"Well . . . I'll tell you who to see. Do you know that Navajo, Tick Hill?"

"Yeah."

"I saw him with some beautiful pieces of silver jewelry. I think he'd sell you one."

"Tick has jewelry?"

"Yep."

"Thanks, Jared!"

Nathan ran down the wooden sidewalk with Tona at his heels. "I've got to buy it before supper time!" he said to the dog. A tall miner, still carrying his dinner pail, came out of the Cherokee just as Nathan reached the saloon.

"Is Tick Hill in there?"

"Who wants to know?" The miner spoke with a thick Welsh accent.

"My name is Nathan Riggins, and I'd like to speak to Mr. Tick Hill, please."

The man jabbed his head back into the saloon and hollered, "Hey, Tick! The Riggins lad is here to see you."

The man turned back and bent low, shoving his face within inches of Nathan's, and the smell of liquor on his breath nearly overpowered the boy. "Don't play poker with that Injun! He's too lucky!" Then the man disappeared down the street.

"You lookin' for me, Riggins?"

Nathan spun around to see the black-vested Tick Hill standing behind him.

"Eh . . . yeah . . . I'm sorry to bother you, but I wanted to buy a fancy silver necklace, and Jared over at the Merc said you had some jewelry for sale."

"I've only got good quality items. You wouldn't be able—"

"I've got five dollars," Nathan interrupted.

Hill lifted his bushy black eyebrows. "It has silver buttons about as big as pennies and a bear claw hanging down in the middle."

"Is . . . is that the kind of necklace a fella gives his girlfriend?"

Tick stepped back and looked Nathan up and down.

"You mean you're buying this for that Walker girl?"

"No! It's for a friend of mine to give to his girl."

"Yeah . . . sure. It's definitely the kind of jewelry a girl would like. Of course, I don't have it on me, and I'm in the middle of a hot streak at the table. How about I bring it over to your house later on?"

"No . . . no!" Nathan protested. "See, I don't really want my parents to find out. It's sort of, you know, a surprise. Could you bring it over to the livery about ten in the morning?"

"All right, I'll be—"

"Hey, Tick, did you hear? I bought William's black horse?"

"That runaway?"

"Yep."

"He's a good horse. You plan on riding tomorrow?"

"Yeah. I want to try him out."

"Let me ride him for about thirty minutes before you climb in the saddle. He's too hot for a kid to jump on right out of the stall."

"Would you do that for me?"

"Nine o'clock . . . at the livery," Hill suggested.

"I'll be there."

With his coat unbuttoned, Nathan skipped all the way home on the already-hard roadway. He scooped up an arm load of wood and burst in through the back door.

"Nathan Timothy!" his mother scolded. "Where have you been all afternoon?"

"Horse shopping. I stopped by to tell you, but I didn't want to wake up Dad, and you were at the meat market."

"Well," she said frowning, "wash your hands and get ready for supper."

"Is Daddy feeling better?"

"He's stiff and sore, but Doc Gooding said it doesn't look infected. He'll be fine."

"He's not going to quit being marshal, is he?" Nathan asked.

"What do you think?"

"I don't think he'd quit for anything."

A rap at the front door caught their attention.

"Nathan, you see who's at the door. I'm going to go wake your father."

The heavy, solid door swung open slowly. Leah Walker, bundled in wool, stood on the porch.

"Hi, Nathan!" she beamed.

"Hi, Leah. What do you need?"

"Me? Oh . . . uh . . . I just thought maybe you wanted to see me," she mumbled.

"About what?"

"I just thought you . . . had . . . you know . . . eh . . . something you wanted to give me."

"Give you? What are you talking about?"

"What I'm talkin' about is that Jared down at the Merc told me you was in lookin' at—" Leah suddenly stopped mid-sentence. "Oh, no! It's that Katie McGregor! It's all them blond curls and that purty pink dress, ain't it?"

Leah ran back down the street as Nathan stared into the quiet coldness of the winter evening.

4

*I*t was not an easy task.

School work.

Chores.

Breakfast.

All before 9:00 A.M.

But somehow Nathan did it.

Tick Hill waited for him at the livery.

"You got the necklace?" Nathan shouted as he ran toward the barn.

"Yep. Made by the finest craftsman between Shiprock and Santa Fe."

"Who's that?"

"My uncle." Tick grinned.

Nathan took the piece in his hand and held it up in the sunlight. The metal was slick and cold. The high degree of polishing caused the entire street of horses, buildings, and busy people to reflect in its beads.

"It's real heavy!" Nathan exclaimed.

"It's real silver," Tick reminded him.

"Five dollars?" Nathan inquired.

"And a horse ride."

Nathan gave the Navajo five dollars and took the necklace.

"Is this a real bear claw?"

"Yep."

"It's bigger than I thought," Nathan added.

"You don't usually get close enough to see them proper." Tick Hill ambled over to the side of the barn. "Is that your saddle?"

"Yeah, the one with the basket weave."

"Well, climb up on the fence, and I'll show you how good a horse you bought."

For the next thirty minutes Nathan, bundled in his warmest coat, and Tona watched a master horseman at work. The big black horse looked frightened and ready to bolt, yet Hill's soothing words and smooth movements kept the horse standing still. He pulled the left rein tight and grabbed the horn as he mounted.

The black horse spun a tight circle to the left. Then suddenly Hill jerked him to the right, and the horse followed his command. He made several loops around the corral and then had Nathan open the gate.

Sprinting behind the livery, the Indian rode the horse straight up the side of the mountain behind Galena. Then he circled some tailings and galloped back to the barn.

Even though they were jammed in his pockets, Nathan's hands were getting cold when Tick offered him the reins.

"Okay, cowboy . . . it's your turn. Just don't let him know you're worried."

Sure. I watched him drag Mr. Williams through town. Well . . . Lord, if I'm going to get busted, it's going to be while tryin'—not hidin'.

To his surprise, the horse neither bucked nor shied, but stood still waiting for Nathan's command.

"You'll be all right," Tick encouraged him. "Until tomorrow morning. You'll have to settle him down until he gets used to being rode every day."

"Yes, sir. Thank you."

"You going for a ride?"

"Yep."

"Well, you might not want to be gone too long. There's a storm rollin' in."

"But it's clear," Nathan commented.

Hill pointed to distant clouds on the western horizon. "It's almost clear. By noon we'll lose the sun, and after that . . . who knows?"

With Tona leading the way, Nathan nudged the black horse's flanks and trotted out of town. For the next two hours the boy held back the reins on the black horse, not wanting to lose control and trying to dodge the wagon ruts, now frozen hard. With his bandanna pulled up over his face and his hands jammed deep in his coat pockets, Nathan crested the rise and looked down on Skeeter's cabin.

The prospect of finally owning the spotted horse excited him, and he lightly spurred the black horse to a faster gait. But panic struck his heart when he realized that the spotted horse was not in the corral, nor was there smoke in the chimney.

"He left!" he shouted at Tona. "He promised he wouldn't leave until noon and . . . he left!"

The horse, sensing some relief from a heavy hand at the bit, galloped toward the cabin with Nathan bouncing dejectedly in the saddle. Out of concern, he stood in the stirrups the last few hundred feet. Tona had circled the cabin by the time Nathan arrived.

While tying the black horse to the rail, he noticed a piece of paper jammed in cracks of the front door of the cabin. Nathan snatched the scrap of rough brown wrinkled paper and stepped out into the yard to read the note. Dark clouds now hung heavy, and vision under the porch was shadowy.

Dear Nate,

I had to ride up the trail to meet a friend, BUT I
WILL BE BACK. It might be a little past noon, so
rest my new horse in the corral, build a fire, and
help yourself to some beans. I'll see you in a little
while with your spotted horse.

Temp

*My spotted horse! I knew it! I knew he wouldn't just ride
off like that! Temple Cholach's the kind of man who will keep
his word!*

"Hey, Tona! It's okay! He's coming back. We'll just warm
up a little first."

Nathan pulled his saddle off the black horse, led it out to
the corral, and tossed it a few flakes of hay. Then he headed for
the cabin. Within moments he had a fire blazing and a small
pot of beans warming. Taking a plate of beans to the door, he
stepped out to feed Tona. But the thin coyote-like dog had disappeared. Nathan left the meal on the porch and retreated to
the fire.

Sometime in the next few minutes, with fire warming his
bones from the outside and beans on the inside, Nathan dozed
off.

■

For a moment, Nathan forgot where he was. The room
was dark and chilly, the fire almost out, and Tona was barking
out in the yard. He had no idea how long he had slept.
Stepping out into the yard, he glanced at the western sky. The
angry black clouds blocked any warmth the sun might have
offered.

His arms shivered in the cold, and he hurriedly pulled on his coat. He could feel goose bumps on his arms and legs.

It must be after two. Mother will be furious.

With his vision clearing, he noticed a rider on a spotted horse galloping towards the cabin. In a matter of minutes, Temple Cholach rode up in the front yard and leaped off the horse.

"Nathan! You waited. That's great! I was afraid that I'd blown the deal. 'Course I wouldn't have blamed you—me being this late and all."

"I gave you my word," Nathan offered.

Cholach began to pull his gear off the still-panting Onepenny. "Listen, I was supposed to meet a friend up on the Paradise Valley trail, but the guy never showed up. I hurried back as fast as I could. Now I'm late getting out of here myself. This storm will cut loose and drop snow on us soon. Did you find a necklace?"

Nathan dug into his saddlebag and pulled out the cloth-wrapped necklace.

"It's beautiful!" Cholach exclaimed. "You've got good taste. Navajo, right?"

"Yes, sir . . . I mean, Temp. It's real silver."

"Well, bring that tall black pony over here and let's make a trade."

For the next several moments they spoke little as they cinched down their own gear to their new mounts. Onepenny, a full hand shorter than the black and much quieter, proved easy for Nathan to saddle.

"Eh . . . Temp . . . could I have a bill of trade on this horse deal?"

"A handshake is good enough for me." Cholach entered the cabin to retrieve the rest of his supplies.

"Well . . . it is for me, too . . . it's just . . . my parents aren't going to believe I traded for such a good horse. It would make it a whole lot easier for me."

"Sure. You draw it up. You can use the back side of that paper I stuck in the door."

Cholach was in the saddle, ready to ride by the time Nathan emerged with the hand-written bill of trade. He signed it and gave it back to Nathan.

"There you go—all legal like."

"Thanks, Mr. Cholach." Nathan beamed.

"Take good care of Onepenny. If I ride through here next spring, I'll stop and see how he is."

"That would be great! Just stop by the marshal's office in Galena. They'll know where to find me."

"The marshal's office?"

"Yeah, didn't I tell you? My dad's the marshal in Galena."

"No foolin'? Now ain't that somethin'?" Cholach grinned. "Listen, Nate, I got two big favors to ask of you. First, keep Onepenny at a walk most of the way home. I'm afraid I tired him out trying not to miss you."

"Right." Nathan pulled his hat down to protect his ears from the stinging cold wind. "What's the other thing?"

"Well . . . I hate to ask you, but I've just got to get a message to this friend of mine who's late. So could you ride up that Paradise Valley trail until you meet up with a short man named Little Jed Walters? Tell him to meet me at the Bar-T in Owyhee County. Look, I know it's a lot to ask, but you could walk Onepenny up the trail. By then he would be rested, and you can run him back to town. Chances are, you'll get home about the same time anyway."

"Actually . . . I, eh . . . yeah, sure. Look for Little Jed and tell him to meet you at the Bar-T?"

"Right. And tell him I've got a horse that will win every

race from Silver City to Fort Hall. I'll see you on down the trail, Nate."

Nathan waved a quick salute as Temple Cholach trotted the black horse to the northeast. Then Nathan mounted up Onepenny. His saddle felt cold, but comfortable. Looking around as if someone might be watching, Nathan patted the spotted horse's rump and then laid across the horn and hugged his neck.

"Boy . . . you now belong to Nathan Timothy Riggins!" He circled the house once before leaving the yard.

It will be dark when I get home. Mom and Dad will . . . of course, I didn't say how long I'd ride up the trail. I could just ride a little while and then turn for town. I think that trail swings close to Willow Springs. Maybe I should stop and see Earl Thunder. I could ride over Lookout Mountain. That would save some miles! Providing the storm holds off.

Nathan rode the spotted horse out to the Paradise Valley trail, still trying to figure a way to get back to Galena before dark. As he rode up the grade, Nathan braced himself against the cold and tried to sort out his thoughts.

Why didn't Mr. Cholach just leave a note for his friend at the cabin? Maybe his friend didn't know he would be staying there. Why did he tell me noon if he knew he would be out on the trail? I hope I'm not late . . . Lord, don't let Mom worry too much. Look, I just didn't find anyone . . . so I'll—

Tona's barking pulled him out of his daydreams, and he glanced up the long slope of the trail to see a very small cabin and a corral about a mile distant.

"Is there a horse in the corral?" he asked Tona. The dog seldom barked at people, but he always barked at animals.

Nathan spotted some movement next to the cabin and hurried Onepenny up the trail.

Maybe that's Little Jed, or whoever!

Suddenly the animal in the corral jumped straight up over the six-foot gate and sprinted up the treeless mountain.

"It's a muley, Tona. It's only a deer!"

Reaching the cabin, he checked inside to find only cobwebs and a broken bunk. The fireplace alone looked useable. He stepped back outside. The air had become instantly white with large flakes, and he couldn't even see the abandoned corral.

"Tona, maybe this is blowing by. I'm going to build a fire and warm up . . . then we'll ride home."

Nathan pulled the saddle and gear off Onepenny and propped it near the fireplace. He led the spotted horse up on the covered porch of the little cabin, took out the bit and headstall, and roped him to a post facing away from the storm.

Next he snatched some straw out of the ripped, homemade mattress in the cabin and gave some to Onepenny. With another handful he made a small nestlike bed for Tona near the horse. He knew the dog would refuse to go indoors.

Blustering his way through the storm, he found that the far side of the corral was broken in pieces, so he gathered up several arm loads of wood and carried them inside. It was such a heavy storm that Nathan couldn't tell if it was midafternoon or almost sunset.

With a fire blazing, he dug through his saddlebags hoping to find something to eat. As he expected, there was no food. But he did find his book about Bonneville. Curling up close to the fire, he opened it up to chapter 28.

Crossing an elevated ridge, Captain Bonneville
now came upon Bear River, which, from its source
to its entrance into the Great Salt Lake, describes
the figure of a horseshoe. . . .

Some time later in the midst of an exciting account about the Digger Indians, Nathan glanced up and realized it was now getting dangerously late in the day. Only flames from the fire lit the room. He figured he'd better start the hard ride back to Galena. Catching one last warm blast from the fire, he dragged his saddle to the door.

Only Onepenny's head and the darkness greeted him.

I knew it! I knew it would be too late! That Jed never showed up, and my folks will be really mad. But they can't make me give the horse back! No sir, I do have the spotted horse!

"Tona, we'll have to wait until morning. You want to come in here where it's warm?"

The dog didn't even open its eyes.

Nathan knew he didn't have enough firewood to last the night, but he figured on using the broken pieces of the bunk, if needed. What concerned him most was not having any supper—and the just anger of his parents.

Sleep soon erased both worries.

■

A low, guttural growl woke Nathan. The room was cold, the floor was hard, his saddle made a stiff pillow, and the fire had softened to a glow. He rolled over and shoved a couple more pieces of the broken bunk into the fire and sat up.

Then he heard the growl again.

Tona? Growling? He only growls like that when . . . when he's cornered by something a lot bigger than he is!

Nathan grabbed his scabbard and pulled out his carbine. He pumped five bullets into the breech but didn't cock the gun.

A bear? There aren't any bears around here. A coyote?

Nah, he always barks at coyotes. I've got to see what it is without it seeing me!

In the dark Nathan crawled on his stomach to the front of the cabin. Then he slowly pulled the rough, splintery door open just a crack. He cocked the carbine and slithered until his head and shoulders were out on the porch.

About two inches of snow blanketed the steps, and he could see Onepenny, still on the porch, with ears tilted toward the corral. Even though it was dark and the storm still raged, Nathan was able to make out a few objects in the reflected glow of the bright snow.

Tona lay on the straw, his head bent to listen to the darkness.

"What is it, boy?" he whispered.

Tona didn't move, but he continued growling.

He's scared. He's really scared!

Nathan waited by the door for a few minutes, but he saw and heard nothing. Realizing that most of the heat was flowing out the open door, he crawled back inside and silently closed the door. He didn't have any way to lock it, so he propped himself against the back wall of the cabin near the fireplace. After stuffing in more wood, he pulled the saddle blanket over his lap and pointed the cocked rifle at the door.

Lord, I'll just have to stay awake until dawn.

He didn't.

■

It wasn't gunfire that woke him in the morning.

It wasn't even the deep growl from Tona.

Instead it was a sharp rap on the front wall of the cabin. Then another . . . and another.

That's not gunfire. Arrows? Are those arrows? There isn't Indian trouble around here, is there?

He was just about to crack the door for a peek when he realized it was breaking day.

Why isn't Tona barking?

Then came another crash at the door, a whinny from Onepenny, and finally a shout. "Ho, the cabin! You're completely surrounded. Put your weapons on the floor, your hands above your hat, and walk out that door. If you shoot, we will be forced to kill you!"

Kill me? Who wants to kill me, Lord?

"Who are you?" Nathan shouted.

"Deputy Haley and posse from Galena. We've got twenty armed men out here, Blueman. We want you out of that cabin right now!"

Deputy Haley? Blueman? They think I'm Colt Blueman, the outlaw?

"Deputy Haley?" Nathan shouted. "Jim? It's me, Nathan Riggins. Don't shoot!"

"Nathan? Is he holding a gun on you, Nate?"

"I'm alone!"

"Where's Blueman?"

"I ain't never seen him!" Nathan hollered.

"His horse is tied to the porch."

"That's my horse! Can I come out now?"

"Come on out, Nate, but don't carry a gun."

"You won't let them shoot me, will ya?"

"No one will shoot."

"Tell all twenty of 'um not to shoot me," Nathan pleaded.

"Nate, come on . . . it's just me, Tick Hill, and two others. That talk about twenty was just a bluff."

Nathan walked out of the cabin into the freezing

December morning and was met in the snow-covered yard by Deputy Haley, Tick Hill, Big Elmer, and O.T. Perry.

"What are you doing here? Your mama's sick with worry. She thinks that black horse drug you all the way to Virginia City by now."

"I got stuck in the storm and sat it out in this cabin."

"Where's your black horse?" Tick asked.

"I traded him. Him and the necklace for the spotted horse."

"You traded that fast horse to Colt Blueman?" Haley asked.

"No, I traded him to a drifting cowboy named Temple Cholach . . . look, I've got a bill of trade. It's official."

"He's got the big black?" Hill pressed.

"Yeah, but he's a nice man. His name is Cholach, see? And he's headed to Owyhee County."

"Well, Tick," Haley said nodding, "wherever Blueman's headed, he's halfway there by now. Our horses are tired and his is fresh."

"I told you, it wasn't Colt Blueman!" Nathan shouted.

"Tall. Thin. Strong shoulders. Thick mustache . . ."

"Lots of men look like that!" Nathan protested.

Deputy Haley set the hammer down on his Winchester and sighed. "Nate, that's Colt Blueman, and yesterday about 10:30 in the morning he stopped the Shiloh stage and robbed them of $20,000 in greenbacks. One of the guards took a bullet in the leg. Then the outlaw rode off on a spotted horse."

"That spotted horse." Tick Hill pointed.

"But . . . but . . . that—this horse is mine!" Nathan insisted.

"That might be," Haley said motioning. "Now mount up and let's get you home before your mama and your daddy die of worry."

Nathan's head and heart were still spinning with words, scenes, and questions when they set out loping down the Paradise Valley/Galena trail.

Tona tagged along far behind the others.

5

*F*or five days the entire town of Galena, Nevada, filed by the livery stable to look at Onepenny. With an occasional flurry of snow still in the air, most tried to dust off the spotted pony's rump, but then finally accepted his colors.

In the minds of people in northern Nevada, the legendary Colt Blueman ranked with Black Bart and Joaquin Murieta. In fear and awe they repeated the tales of his supposed robberies and exploits.

Nathan, the only one in town who had met the man, became the center of attention because he owned what was assumed to be Blueman's spotted horse. Several times a day Nathan would ride Onepenny up and down the streets of Galena, demonstrating the horse's many tricks.

Within a week, Nathan's father, now able to get back in the saddle, received considerable information about Colt Blueman.

"Look at this!" Marshal Riggins tossed three telegrams on the dinner table as he sat down with Nathan and his mother to eat. "A sheriff near Santa Fe wired to say that Blueman had robbed a bank north of there last Tuesday in a town called Tres Casas. But here is another telegram from Lewiston, Idaho, saying Blueman held up the Florence stage on Monday! And this guy," he pointed to the third telegram, "says he shot and killed

Blueman in Big Trouble, Montana, last June, and he wants someone to forward the reward money!"

"How do you know which to believe?" Nathan asked. "What if Temple Cholach isn't Blueman at all?"

"I believe it was Blueman," his father insisted. "He took the Shiloh money and is laying low. All this hysteria about him just helps him hide."

"Then maybe he isn't all that far away?" Nathan asked.

"Maybe not. Look, between us and the next town to the east is about two hundred miles of wilderness without a soul in it or a road through it. Every fifty feet there is a dandy place to hide. There's no way to find Blueman until he shows up in a town somewhere."

"So you're not going to chase Cholach . . . or Blueman . . . or whoever?"

"Nope."

"What if he comes to town?"

"I'll arrest him, but he won't come to Galena."

"Why not?"

"You're here. You're about the only one in northern Nevada who knows what he looks like. He'll avoid Galena like a gambler avoids church."

"Doesn't someone have to chase him down?"

"Oh, the U.S. Marshal will take on the chase if they ever get caught up with their other business," Marshal Riggins replied.

Nathan paced the room, finally peering out at a clear sky. "Dad, a chinook's blowin' in."

"I reckon it is."

"Well, since it's warming up, and I've got my homework all done until Miss D'Imperio returns, can I take Onepenny out to Skeeter's cabin and just look around for some clues? I mean,

I know that Cholach was out there several days. Maybe he left something in the cabin to prove he is Blueman."

"Nothin' of consequence is out there. Deputy Haley already checked."

"I know, but it gives me someplace to ride to," Nathan pleaded.

"I suppose it would keep folks from pestering the livery for a gawk at that spotted horse. You'd just ride out and back?"

"Yep."

"What do you think, Adele?"

Nathan's mother set down her coffee cup.

"Chinook or not, you take a bedroll and matches," she lectured. "Last time you went out there you got snowed in."

Within minutes Nathan was in the saddle riding One-penny down the main street of Galena. Tona meandered about ten steps ahead of them.

"Nathan! Where are you going? Are you going for a ride? Are you going to Skeeter's cabin? Can I go with you? Nathan? Can I go? Please!"

He glanced over at Leah who was skipping parallel to him on the wooden sidewalk.

"Leah, you can't go."

"Why cain't I?"

"It isn't proper."

"What do you mean, it ain't proper?"

"Someone might think you're my girlfriend. Last I can remember, you aren't my girlfriend."

"No, I ain't your girlfriend. And you didn't give no silver necklace to Katie McGregor neither. But I ain't going to marry you. I ain't going to marry nobody but Kylie Collins!"

"Exactly," Nathan said triumphantly. "So that's why you're not going on this trip."

"You think you're so smart! Well, you ain't so smart, Nathan T. Riggins!" she shouted as he turned to put the wind at his back.

■

It was midmorning when Nathan reached the cabin. He wasn't sure what he was looking for, but he knew he hadn't found it.

Most of this stuff belongs to Skeeter. The newspapers tacked to the walls to stop the drafts are too old to belong to Cholach . . . or Blueman . . . or whatever his name is.

The sagging floorboards of the cabin creaked as Nathan rattled back out to the porch. He slipped off his coat and tied it to the cantle. Then he mounted and rode around the cabin watching for Cholach's tracks. Tona zigzagged beside them for a while, but the continual circles puzzled him, so he finally slumped down in front of the cabin and watched.

I know this is the way to find his tracks . . . but what with the snow last week, I can't tell one track from another. I wish I could track like Tick Hill . . . Lord, it's not right for Cholach to get away with robbing the stage! Somebody needs to catch him, but everyone's too busy with other problems. Now, Lord, I know I'm just a kid, but he tricked me . . . I provided him with that fast horse. So I was thinkin' it sure would be good if I found him and turned him in. It's kind of like I owe it to the folks whose money was stolen.

Nathan felt good about praying and half expected to open his eyes and find a sign of Blueman's direction.

But he didn't.

There was nothing at all.

About two hundred feet beyond the cabin he decided to

give up and return to Galena. Dropping the reins on the saddle horn, he stretched around to whistle to Tona. When he turned back, he didn't grab the reins but just punched Onepenny with his spurs and hollered, "Let's go home, Onepenny. Let's go home!"

The horse started a slow trot towards the east. It took Tona's barking before Nathan realized what had happened.

"Wait! Wrong way, boy . . . Galena's to the west . . . wait! Tona, maybe Onepenny is going home—to his home with Cholach!"

Nathan circled the horse around the cabin once more and stopped by the porch. Again he dropped the reins, spurred the horse, and called out, "Go home, Onepenny. Go home!"

Again the spotted horse started east, and again Tona excitedly tried to direct the horse back to the Galena trail.

"No, Tona! Leave him alone. He is going home . . . to his old home!"

Nathan had barely cleared the yard when Tona suddenly left them and darted up the Galena trail.

"Tona! We aren't going that way . . . Tona!"

Then in the distance Nathan spotted the source of Tona's sudden excitement.

Someone's coming up the trail!

Standing in the stirrups, Nathan stared at the approaching rider until he recognized the profile.

"Leah!" he shouted. "What are you doing out here?"

"I'm just going for a ride." She sniffed as she drew closer. "Fancy meetin' you here."

"You knew I was coming to Skeeter's."

"And you knew I wanted to come along."

"Yes, and I didn't invite you."

"Well," she said glowing, "I'm here."

"I'm going home," Nathan announced.

"Really?"

Nathan pushed his hat back. "Nah, I mean, I was. Then I told Onepenny to go home, and he headed toward the east. I think he might be going home to Cholach's place."

"So . . . what are we going to do?" Leah asked.

"I'm going to let Onepenny lead for a while and see if there are any traces of Cholach and that black horse."

"Well," she informed him, "*I'm* going that way too!"

Leah dropped in behind Nathan and followed at a short distance. Tona tried his best to get Onepenny off his trail and back on the road to Galena.

"Tona, quit barking!" Nathan shouted.

When they reached a steep descent into a dry creekbed, Tona became insistent that they turn back. Onepenny finally just stopped and refused to go further on his own.

"What's the matter?" Leah called.

"Tona's being a pest. Now Onepenny won't go on without following my lead, and I have no idea which way Cholach went."

"What are you going to do?" she asked.

"I know what I should do. I should take Tona back to Galena and lock him in the woodshed."

"But it would be the middle of the afternoon before we got back out here," she argued.

Nathan suddenly spun Onepenny back towards Skeeter's cabin. "Come on!" he shouted. He raced to the corral with Leah and Tona trailing behind.

By the time Leah arrived, Nathan was exiting the cabin with an empty flour sack in his hand and a coil of twine clenched in his teeth. He turned the sack inside out and shook it in the wind.

"Nathan Riggins, what ya doin'?"

He ignored Leah and called Tona. He grabbed the dog,

wrestled his head, scratched his back, rubbed his stomach, and then with a sudden jerk, he pulled the flour sack up over Tona. In a matter of seconds, Nathan had tied the sack loosely around Tona's neck.

"You sacked him?" Leah gasped.

"Maybe he won't be such a nuisance."

"He won't like it," Leah shouted above the frantic barking of the dog.

"Obviously," Nathan hollered, "but maybe Onepenny will go on in his own way now."

With the barking dog bagged except for its head and lying across the front of the saddle, Nathan mounted and roared, "Onepenny, go home!"

The horse cranked his neck back toward the yapping dog and refused to move. Even Nathan's spurs couldn't ignite the horse.

"It ain't no use," Leah howled, "we've got to take that dog home."

"Not *WE* . . . but *YOU!*" Nathan announced.

"Me? That ain't my dog," she protested.

"Well, this isn't your horse either. And I need to follow this trail awhile before he forgets the way to Cholach's. Leah, I'm askin' you real nice—would you please take Tona back and lock him in the woodshed? Then tell Dad what I'm doing. I think he and the others might be interested in this. They'll probably want to come out here and take up the pursuit."

"Can I come back with them?"

"Yep."

"How will I know the trail you're on?"

"I'll mark it."

"How?"

"I'll break sage and pile some rocks along the way. You

won't miss it. Besides, Dad and Tick Hill will be able to spot it. Will you do it?"

"You got to promise two things," she demanded.

"What?"

"You have to promise that you won't never go around town sayin' that I'm your girlfriend."

Nathan nodded. "Okay, I'll never tell folks that you're my girlfriend. What's the other thing?"

"You gotta promise that you won't never tell folks I ain't your girlfriend neither."

Nathan pushed back his hat and ran his fingers through his brown hair. "You mean I can't tell them you are my girlfriend, and I can't tell them you aren't my girlfriend?"

"Yep. Do you promise on a stack of Bibles?" she demanded.

"Eh . . . I don't think I ought to bring a Bible into this, but my promise is good. You know that."

"Okay, but you owe me a favor, Nathan T. Riggins. And I aim to collect."

"Yeah," Nathan mumbled, "I'm sure you will. Listen, you ride on out of here. When you're out of sight, then I'll see if I can get Onepenny going again."

Leah started out of the yard.

"Nate." She scrunched her nose and squinted as she looked back. "Be careful!"

Nathan stared at her brown eyes for a long moment. "Leah . . . eh, thanks . . . you're a good friend."

"But I ain't your girlfriend," she blurted out.

He started to reply and then paused for a second. "I'm not sayin' yes and I'm not sayin' no," he finally replied.

A big grin swept over Leah's face. "And neither am I." She giggled and rode up the trail towards Galena.

Once Leah was out of sight, Nathan dropped the reins

and kicked Onepenny with his spurs and called out, "Go home, Onepenny . . . come on, let's go home!"

The spotted horse trotted back down the eastern trail he had scouted earlier, and soon Nathan was descending into the dry creekbed. He had expected the horse to cross the sandy creek bottom and climb the other side. Instead, Onepenny loped along the dry stream angling off to the south.

How do I know if Onepenny is headed home or if he's just wandering around? I'd better keep this trail marked so I can find my way home.

Rather than waste time to stop and eat dinner when the sun was straight up, Nathan dug some biscuits out of his saddlebags and kept riding. Even the noontime sun on this mild day didn't completely warm him, so by early afternoon he had pulled on his coat.

Onepenny led him down out of the hills, out of the creekbed, and into a long valley. The landscape was punctuated by wave after wave of gray-blue sage and dry arroyos. As far as Nathan knew, there were no towns, gold claims, or even major trails out in this region. But he did know that if he went far enough, he would reach the Utah white desert. He had no intention of going that far.

"Onepenny?" The horse's ears shot straight up when Nathan spoke. "If we don't find some trace soon, maybe we ought to think about going back. Maybe Cholach did swing around and ride north to Idaho. I mean, this might be the way you and he came in . . . but not the way he left!"

As Nathan rode across the valley, he was surprised to see a steep barranca that had been invisible on the horizon only a few steps before. The spotted horse plunged over the edge of the cliff, and Nathan held on as they descended to the bottom. Then Onepenny turned north for a couple hundred feet and came halfway up the barranca to a flat shelf of alluvial soil.

The back wall of the plateau held a large, semicircular cave. A ring of ashes marked the place where a campfire had been.

"Is this where he stopped, boy? Not a bad spot. You can't see it from the valley, and there is some protection from the storm."

Deciding to give Onepenny a rest, Nathan climbed down and loosened the cinch on his horse. Tying him to some leafless brush that surrounded the shelf, Nathan leaned up against a rock and rested.

He had just closed his eyes when he heard Onepenny whinny. Nathan sat straight up and searched the landscape. Walking slowly, he approached Onepenny and pulled his rifle from the scabbard. Pumping in exactly five cartridges, he returned to the cave at the back of the clearing.

Within moments, Nathan heard hoofbeats on the rocky, dry streambed at the bottom of the barranca. Then the leafless brush shuddered, and finally a gray horse and sombrero-topped rider emerged.

Nathan cocked his carbine and pointed it at the approaching rider, who turned out to be leading another gray horse laden with gear.

"Ho, in the bushes!" Nathan called.

The bearded man in the silver-trimmed saddle flung a startled glance at Nathan.

"*¿Niño? ¿Qué es esto?*" The man waved his hand at the cave and the flat shelf of smooth dirt.

"I don't speak Mexican. Do you speak English?" Nathan asked, keeping his hand on his carbine.

"*¿Cómo se llama?*"

"I said, I don't speak Mexican," Nathan called out.

"*¿Dónde va usted?*"

Nathan walked slowly to Onepenny and tightened the

cinch without taking an eye off the man. He climbed aboard and started back down the barranca to the earlier trail.

"*Hijo, hay mucho oro aquí . . . no?*"

"Look, I told you . . . '*mucho oro?*'" Nathan paused. "Much gold? There's gold here?"

The dark-skinned man smiled and pointed at his gold front tooth. "*Sí. Oro . . . eh . . . ¿cómo se dice? . . .* gold *aquí! ¿Este es el . . . el . . .* claim *de usted?*"

Nathan searched his mind to understand the man. "Claim? Gold claim? My gold claim? No . . . eh . . . no!"

The man pushed his hat back and revealed a weather-wrinkled face. "*Es bueno! Este es el . . .* eh . . . claim *de* Miguel Linasto Garcia!"

Nathan waved his right hand toward the cave, tipped his hat, and started to ride off. Then he remembered Cholach and suddenly spun Onepenny around towards the Mexican who had now dismounted and was sifting through the dirt at the entrance to the cave.

"Señor?" Nathan felt awkward at trying to speak Spanish.

"*Sí?*"

"Did you see a man on fast, black horse?"

The man just stared at Nathan.

"Did you see . . . eh, a . . . *un hombre* . . . on a black, eh . . . *caballo* . . . a fast, black *caballo?*

This isn't working. He doesn't have any idea what I'm . . . Lord, why can't I remember any of those words Miss D'Imperio taught us? Black? Rojo is red. Azure is blue. Blanco is white. Negro!

"*Caballo negro! Un hombre* and a fast, *un rapido caballo negro?*"

The man turned and took two steps towards Nathan.

"*No vi un hombre.*"

67

"You didn't see him? Or, you didn't see anyone?"

The man only shrugged.

"How about a house? A *casa*? A farm? A ranch?"

Then, waving his arms back down the barranca, the man explained, "*Uno rancho es un dia del sur.*"

"One day . . . eh . . . that way?" Nathan pointed in the same direction as the man.

"*Sí!*"

"Thank you . . . eh, *gracias!*" Nathan shouted.

Nathan rode back down the little canyon to where the trail had dropped off into the steep-walled, brush-laden creekbed, and then he climbed up the far side to the valley floor. The climb was so vertical that he clutched the horn with both hands to keep from sliding out of the saddle.

"Well, Onepenny, something is only a day away! Go home, Onepenny, go home!"

Once again the spotted horse trotted down the trail with the reins lying free on his mane.

6

Did he actually say that Cholach was one day south? Maybe it's another black horse. Or was it a black house? Perhaps Cholach is riding south himself. If so, he will always be a day ahead of me! If he's riding north, we could meet! What if he is Colt Blueman?

For the first time since the journey began, Nathan started to worry about what he would do if he did, indeed, find Temple Cholach. Nathan had met an outlaw once before, Lexie Devere, and had survived only with help from his friends and from God.

Finally he decided that if he discovered Cholach's hideout, he would wait for his father and the others to catch up with him.

If they don't show up by morning, I'll go back to Galena and draw them a map to Cholach's, provided I can follow my own trail backwards.

When the sun began to dip in the western sky, Nathan suddenly had an additional worry.

I'm not going to find him in one day, and it's a long way back to Skeeter's cabin . . . of course if Dad's on his way . . . but maybe Leah got lost going home. If she didn't git the message to Dad, I'll be in trouble again! My parents are really going to be mad this time! Of course, I've got my bedroll . . . but I don't want to be outdoors if the temperature drops . . .

Lord, a nice little cabin tucked out of the wind would suit me fine. Actually a cave might work.

Nathan hadn't seen even the ruins of a building since he left Skeeter's cabin, and he hadn't viewed a person since he left the Mexican prospector. Taking up the reins, he rode One-penny off his course and up to the top of a small smooth hill that lay like bread dough in the middle of the prairie.

He stood up on his saddle and peered in every direction, but he could see no signs of buildings or life. It was still clear, but the setting sun seemed to be taking what warmth there was with it.

Dropping back into the saddle, he patted the spotted horse. The horse stretched his neck to glance back at Nathan. "Onepenny, we're going to have to make camp out here. Then we will go half a day further. The Mexican said something was one day south, and about noon tomorrow will make one day. If we don't find Cholach by then, we're going home—to our real home!"

Deciding that the east slope of the hill would provide as much protection as he could find, Nathan stopped beside a large clump of sagebrush and dismounted. The tall sage had offered some shade during the summer months, and a small patch of dried grass provided a little food for Onepenny.

Although it was still an hour before dark, Nathan hurried to the tedious job of collecting scrappy firewood from the dead lower branches of sage. Finally deciding he had enough for the night, he built his fire. He tied off Onepenny's lead rope to a heavy rock the size of a boot. Then Nathan crawled inside his bedroll and began to dig through his saddlebag for supper.

Night came with a legion of bright stars flung against a ceiling of black. *Tona ought to be here. That's what I need. He's got the eyes and ears for the night. Well, at least it's clear and not too cold.*

He considered leaving a stiff fire to signal his father where he was camped, but decided that it could be a signal to others as well. Nathan slid down deep in the bedroll, pulled the canvas tarp up and over his head, and shoved his carbine, scabbard and all, down inside the blankets with him. He pushed five bullets into the breech and drifted off to sleep.

Somewhere in the middle of a grand dream about riding Onepenny in front of a grandstand full of cheering people, Nathan rolled over to wipe his nose on his sleeve and realized that it was beginning to rain. Partially hidden under his blankets and canvas bedroll, he peeked out to see no stars, yet he felt the increasing tempo of a cold rain.

But it was clear! There wasn't a cloud in the sky!

Lightning flashed over the western mountains, with thunder following a few seconds behind. Rain, sleet, and snow blew wildly across the valley.

I'm stuck here until daylight. I'd go home if I could find my way. Well, I don't have to worry about a sneak attack. No man or animal would be stupid enough to come out on a night like this. No one but me!

Nathan stoked the heavily smoking fire with as much dry wood as he could salvage, scooted back into his bedroll, and watched as the lightning crept closer to camp. The rain pelted and stung Nathan's face. The fire didn't help. He had just pulled the canvas tarp over his head completely blocking vision when the lightning and thunder crashed at the exact same time overhead, and the inside of his bedroll lit up like it had lantern light.

Onepenny whinnied and snorted. Nathan started to get out and settle the horse when a second, third, and fourth peel of lightning caused him to dive back under the covers.

He won't scare easy. Onepenny could probably take better care of me than I could of him.

Nathan scrunched down under the covers and pulled on his boots that had been inside his bedroll in order to keep them free from bugs. He could feel the water soaking through the blankets to his trousers. He wiggled around searching for dry corners in his blankets and tried to go back to sleep. The next two crashes of thunder struck somewhere to the east. Nathan knew that the lightning had passed over and was headed for the distant hills.

Heavy rain followed, and slowly he felt the wetness soak all his clothing. First it was the right side of his trousers, then his shoulders, then his back, then the rest of his trousers, then most of his coat.

Snow is a lot dryer. I wish that it would go ahead and snow . . . you can keep a fire going in a snow storm! Where will I find dry wood to build a fire and dry out my gear in the morning? If it's still raining, I'm just going to ride home wet. This is really stupid. I don't need to be out here. I could be home in my bed. . . . Lord, this is Nathan . . . You see, I was really mad at Cholach for making me seem like a dumb kid who can't tell a cowboy from an outlaw. So I figured I ought to get even with him for suckering me along, but to tell the truth, all I'm getting is wet.

The only two times Nathan began to doze off, the chatter of his teeth woke him up. All through the long hours he kept looking out from under the canvas just long enough to be pricked by the rain, but each time he was disappointed to see no sign of daybreak.

The rain was just a very light, cold drizzle when the eastern sky first hinted of gray. It had stopped altogether when Nathan determined to haul out of bed and try to start a fire.

His clothes hung heavy with water, and his bedroll was a muddy mess. His arms were purple and bumpy. He could keep neither his knees nor his teeth from trembling.

Glancing over at the puddle of water that had been a grassy knoll the night before, Nathan stared at the sage. As if disoriented, he searched around the ground were he was standing and looked back up at the sage.

"Onepenny? . . . Onepenny!" he shouted.

The spotted horse was nowhere in sight.

Nathan sloshed his way over to where he had left Onepenny picketed to the rock.

He wouldn't run away! He's not that type. Is he? The lightning was close but . . . how? . . . why?

A shallow, narrow trench curved down the hillside from the spot where Onepenny last stood.

"The rock!" Nathan shouted. "He's still dragging the rock!"

Nathan turned to grab his gear, and the stiff western breeze hit his wet clothing. He had a sudden urge just to curl up in the mud and try to sleep.

I've got to have a fire . . . Lord, this is serious! Help me!

Most of the scraps of wood he had gathered the night before lay in water or mud. Still trembling, he ran circles around his camp snapping off any dead sage twigs that looked halfway dry. Yanking out a soiled and crinkled scrap of paper that had been wrapped around the jerky in his saddlebags, Nathan scratched out a little fire that was mainly glow and smoke. With his hands and knees in the mud, he bent low and softly blew on the fire.

Lord, this has got to work . . . please, Lord. If this doesn't work . . .

Nathan realized he battled for his life. There was no alternate plan. The thick, gray smoke swirled upwards, stinging his eyes and hanging low because of the heaviness of the air. One branch after another began to glow, then with his careful blowing, caught fire and blazed.

Thank you, Lord!

It took at least twenty minutes for the flames to overtake the smoke and an hour before he felt warm enough to remove some of his wet clothing and hang it out to dry.

I need to find Onepenny. I can't go on all soaking wet . . . I've got to carry my saddle and gear. I should have tied him better in a storm. Even good horses can get spooked . . . I'm just going to find Onepenny and go home.

His long underwear finally dry, Nathan slipped back on his trousers, shirt, and heavy coat. They, too, were dry, but smelled of campfire smoke.

He hung his saddlebags over his shoulder, placed his scabbard around his neck, tied his bedroll and saddle blanket (which were still wet) to the back of the cantle, and hefted the saddle across his shoulders, holding the stirrups in each hand.

He hated to leave the fire, but the threatening clouds warned of rain or snow, and he had exhausted the supply of burnable material in the area.

Onepenny's trail was easy to follow. He had dragged the rock through the mud across the valley floor. Nathan was surprised to see that the horse had changed his southerly direction and now advanced straight east towards some low-lying hills. Nathan's progress was painstakingly slow due to the mud built up on his boots and the weight of the saddle crushing his back.

As he reached the first of the small hills, he noticed that Onepenny had turned south again. Suddenly Nathan spotted a small, two-story house, a barn, and a set of corrals.

That's why he turned off the trail! He was going toward Cholach's in the storm and must have known there was shelter over here. Maybe these people know Cholach!

The old house was unpainted. The yard was just bare dirt, and the barn boards were warped.

"Man, I hope somebody's home!" Nathan grumbled to

himself. He thought he heard horses in the barn, but none could be seen in the corral. Onepenny's trail went straight for the barn door, but Nathan was afraid to follow without checking at the house first.

With a great moan of relief, he slid the saddle down off his shoulders and balanced it on a swaying tie rail in front of the house. His saddlebags still hung from his shoulder, as did his carbine, when he clomped across the porch and knocked at the front door. The threshold stood a good two feet higher than the porch. Steps that at one time had led up to the front door were now missing. Nathan knew that whoever opened the door would tower above him.

He knocked several times on the weathered wood.

"Ho . . . in the house! Can you hear me?"

After a moment he heard a woman's voice.

"Who is it?"

"Ma'am, I'm Nathan T. Riggins from Galena."

"What do you want?"

"Well . . . my horse ran off in that lightning storm, and I'm just trying to chase him down. I think he might have ended up in your barn."

Suddenly the front door flung open, and a tall thin woman with dark wavy hair hanging over her ears stood above him.

"Well, cowboy," she said smiling, "you look a little worse for wear. Would you like to come in and have a hot bowl of soup?"

"Yes, ma'am, I would," he replied, "but could I first run out and check the barn to see if my horse is there?"

"Surely." She smiled.

As Nathan turned to the barn, he heard the lady shout, "Tashawna, you put on that pretty dress. We've got company for dinner."

Onepenny's muddy trail led to sagging double doors that stood partially open. Inside, Nathan found two driving horses in stalls on one side and Onepenny standing in an open stall on the other, his lead rope still attached to the rock.

"Onepenny! I'm really glad to see you!"

He hugged the horse, removed the lead rope, tossed him some nearby hay, and closed the stall gate. Then he ran back to the house.

The door stood open still, and he pulled himself up into the home.

"Did you find him?" the woman at the cookstove asked.

"Yes, ma'am! He must have got confused and just wandered in here last night."

"Well, I am surprised to have a visitor today. This ranch is so remote we seldom see anyone." She placed a bowl of steaming soup and a hunk of fresh-baked bread beside him.

"Oh, here's Tashawna. Did you say your name was Nathaniel?"

"N-Nathan," he stammered.

"Well, this is my daughter, Tashawna."

Nathan turned to see a girl about his age clothed in a long green and white dress, with dark curly hair cascading to her shoulders, a green ribbon in her hair, and a wide smile on her face.

"Hi!" She grinned and then sat down at the table.

Nathan suddenly realized that he was just standing there, not saying anything, and that somehow his mouth had dropped open.

"Oh . . . hello!" he blurted out. "I'm Nathan T. Riggins from Galena."

"Glad to meet you, Nathan. What outfit do you ride for? Maybe the Double S?"

Nathan caught the sparkle in her eyes and almost asked

her what caused such a glow. Her ankles were thin, as were her wrists. Her cheeks showed color as though she spent days outside in the cold. Her smile reminded him of Melissa back in Indiana.

But this smile is ten times cuter than Melissa's.

"I said," she repeated, "who do you ride for? Mother said you were a cowboy."

"Oh . . . hi!" he gulped. "My name's Nathan. She was just joking. I'm not a cowboy . . . yet." He sat down next to Tashawna and smiled at his bowl of soup.

"Did you say you live in Galena?" she asked.

"Eh . . . yeah . . . where do you live?" he mumbled.

"Here."

Nathan could feel his face flush. "Oh . . . yeah . . . what I mean is . . . just where is this? I got sort of lost during the storm."

"Well, some say this is Eureka County, and some say it is Elko County, so I guess you can take your pick."

"You mean, they don't know?"

"Oh, I guess somebody somewhere knows."

Nathan ate some soup. Then he glanced back at Tashawna. "How long have you lived here?" he finally asked.

"Several years, but we're going to move as soon as Daddy gets home. He says that this house is just too cold in the winter. We're going to buy a house in Carson City. Won't that be wonderful? Imagine living in a big city."

"Galena's a nice town," Nathan encouraged her.

"Oh, yes . . . I know," Tashawna replied. "My daddy says it's a long, hard day's ride straight west. Me and Mama only go with him when he takes the wagon into Austin. But we all decided on Carson City."

"Well, I've never been there, but my father says it's a very nice place. In fact, he has mentioned moving there or to Virginia City."

I wonder if I could talk my parents into moving? It makes sense to move now before the winter gets worse. I'll bet he could still get a job with the U.S. Marshal's office.

"My daddy says that Virginia City is too wild a place for a girl to grow up—what with shootings and fights and everything."

"Oh . . . yeah . . . he's probably right . . . it wouldn't be a good place for a girl like you."

"What do you mean 'a girl like me?'" she quizzed.

"One that's . . . eh, you know . . . it's just that you are . . . you know what I mean."

She laid down her spoon, tilted her head, and looked him in the eyes. "No. What do you mean?"

"I mean, it's just that you're so . . . so . . . you're so pretty!" He turned back to stare at his soup bowl and jammed a whole spoonful of steaming hot soup in his mouth and swallowed it quickly. He could feel it burn all the way down. Nathan never looked back at Tashawna nor said anything more until he finished his meal.

She thinks I'm a fool! I am a fool! I've got to go home. I want to go home!

He ignored Tashawna and looked at her mother. "Thanks for dinner, ma'am. I need to get my horse and be heading home. You sure have been generous."

"Well, Nathan, I'd invite you back to visit, but we really are planning on leaving soon."

"Eh . . . what kind of work does your husband do?"

"He buys, sells, and trains horses. That's where he is now. He went up to Idaho to sell some horses to the army."

"Well, I just bought a new horse, and boy is he something!" Nathan bragged. "You ought to come out and let me show you his tricks!"

"I love horses. Let's go see him," Tashawna suggested.

"You put on some shoes and pull on your heavy coat . . . it's cold out there," her mother reminded her.

Nathan stepped down out of the house onto the front porch and tipped his hat to the woman. Then he gathered his gear and tossed his saddle on his shoulder.

Tashawna bolted out the front door and stepped out near the rail. "I'll race you." She giggled.

"But I'm carrying all this!" he protested.

"Well, I'm just a girl," she said laughing.

There was no way Nathan could run anywhere, let alone win a race. He didn't even try.

Tashawna burst into the barn and then suddenly let out a cry of delight. She burst back out into the yard.

"Daddy's home!" She ran around to the corrals searching for something, but she came back just as Nathan kicked open the barn door.

"Your horse ain't in there. He must have wandered off again," she called. "I don't know where Daddy could be, unless he went out hunting on foot."

"Not in here?" He hurried into the barn. "There he is! He's in the stall on the other side!"

"That isn't your horse. That's my daddy's!" she protested.

"I know my horse when I see it."

"No, it isn't. That's Onepenny, and he belongs to my—"

"Onepenny is my horse!"

Her daddy? No . . . no . . .

"Is your daddy's name Temple Cholach?"

"Yes! And I'm Tashawna Cholach."

7

This is Cholach's place! If he catches me here . . .

"Eh . . . you know . . . I bought this horse from your father!"

"You didn't either! My daddy would never sell Onepenny."

"He did too!"

"You're a liar!"

"I am not!" Nathan fumbled in his shirt pocket and waved a folded piece of brown paper in her face. "Look! Here's the bill of trade!"

Tashawna pursed her lips slowly. "Trade?"

"Yeah, I traded your father a fast black horse and a—"

The necklace? For his girlfriend? I can't tell Tashawna that her father has a girlfriend!

"And what else?" she asked.

"Eh . . . like I said, we traded horses."

"Let me see that note." She pulled it out of his hands.

"My daddy didn't write this!"

"I wrote it. Your father signed it. That's his signature."

"Why's it so hard to read?" She brushed back her bangs that had looped down to her eyes.

"It got wet in the storm."

Tashawna stomped back outside with the note still in her

hand. The cold drift of air caused her breath to fog as she spoke. "What does this part say?" she questioned. "A neck brace?"

"Look . . . we traded horses. He got a very fast ink-black horse and I got Onepenny."

"When did he do this?"

"Eh . . . last week. See the date?" Nathan shoved his hat to the back of his head. It caught the cold breeze, and he immediately yanked it tight.

Waving the note at him, she continued, "Then why didn't he come home yet?"

Lord, I don't even know if Cholach's coming home! Maybe he ran off and isn't coming back.

"Look, all I know is that he said he was headed north. Anyway, I'm just going to mount up Onepenny and go home."

Nathan marched back towards the barn, his spurs jingling.

"Where're you going?" She hurried to catch up.

"To saddle up."

"Can . . . can I show this note to my mama?"

If I give her the note, she could go in there and tear it up. Then they'd claim they still own Onepenny, and nobody around here would know different.

"Well?" she insisted. One arm was braced on her hip; the other hung by her side.

Nathan glanced over to see a small tear at the corner of her eye slide across her smooth cheek and soak into her shining dark hair. She reached out and held on to Nathan's arm.

"Yeah . . . show it to your mother. Then bring it to me in the barn. I'm loading up."

The leather saddle felt cold, slick, and hard. Onepenny waited in his stall. The gentle mixture of smells—fresh hay and old manure—reminded Nathan of his grandfather's barn in Indiana.

"So this is home, huh, boy? Well, not any more. Your home is in Galena. And you won't have to rob coaches or banks or anything. Let's get out of here!"

His saddle was set, and he had positioned his scabbard and saddlebags when Tashawna walked up quietly behind him.

"Nathan?"

The voice startled him in a strange way that tingled his throat. He looked around to see her staring at the ground.

"Nathan, my mama says I should apologize for sounding snotty about Onepenny. She said that was Daddy's signature, and if he traded the spotted horse, it was for a good reason. I really like Onepenny. I just didn't think Daddy would do this."

"Listen!" Nathan reached out to touch the shoulder of her brown wool coat that covered the green dress and then immediately jerked his hand back. "You know you can always come to Galena and ride him! Really, it would be fun to have you visit, and you could meet my friends Colin and Leah. Leah's, eh, she's a real true friend and—"

"Is Leah your girlfriend?" Tashawna asked.

Nathan felt uneasy about her eyes fixed on his.

"No . . . I don't have . . ."

Oh, man. Leah should definitely never meet Tashawna!

"No, I don't have a girlfriend."

"Well, we're movin' to Carson City anyway. So I probably won't see you again." She twisted her wavy dark hair in her fingers. "Nathan, could I ride Onepenny around the yard one more time?"

"Yeah, go ahead, but I haven't cinched him too tight."

Tashawna jerked hard on the cinch and led Onepenny out of the barn. She quickly swung up into the saddle and hiked her dress, revealing her boots and long underwear on her legs below her knees. Her coat looked bulky, and she wore no hat.

She kicked Onepenny and began to trot in increasingly wider circles between the barn and the house. She then dropped the reins and, to Nathan's amazement, stood up in the saddle, continuing to ride the horse at a trot. Holding her hands out for balance, she suddenly spun in the saddle and was standing backwards as the horse continued its circular pattern.

Coming close to Nathan, she hollered, "I can stand on my hands, too, but Daddy says it ain't proper in front of boys!"

"Yeah, I can do that, too," Nathan insisted.

Plopping back down in the saddle, she circled the barn, disappearing from Nathan's sight. Then he saw Onepenny gallop from the far side of the barn.

She fell off! No . . . she's riding Indian! She's hiding on the far side, grabbing his neck. She can't jump him that way! Nobody can jump a horse like that. She'll bust her head . . . she did it! Nobody will believe this!

She reined up Onepenny next to Nathan, her face red from the cold wind and her once well-combed hair now mussed up.

"Can you do that?"

"I've jumped him. But I never thought about trying it Indian-style. Tashawna, that was really good riding!"

She leaned over in the saddle and, with a quick jerk, snatched his hat. "Yeah, it was, wasn't it? Wait until you see this one!"

"My hat!" His ears felt the cold sting of the wind.

"You'll get it back!" She giggled.

She rode to the center of the yard and leaned over, tossing the hat, brim up, on the ground. Then she rode down the trail away from the barn and turned to face the yard. Nathan saw her swing her left foot free and pull that stirrup up by hand until it crossed her lap. Then she locked her wrist into the stirrup like it was a handhold.

Kicking Onepenny, she brought him to a full gallop. As she reached the yard, she leaned far to the right side of the saddle, holding on with only her left hand in the stirrup. As she approached the waiting hat, she fell to the right so far Nathan was sure she would lose her grip and be trampled under the hooves of the horse.

She wasn't.

She neatly grabbed his hat on the fly and continued galloping across the yard. Pulling herself back up into the saddle, she spun around to Nathan.

"I believe you dropped your hat, cowboy." She laughed.

"Uh . . . yeah . . . th-thanks!" he stuttered.

We're moving to Carson City! We've got to move to Carson City. Lord, you'll just have to convince Mom and Dad!

"Nathan?" Tashawna was on the ground, handing him the reins.

"Oh . . . listen," Nathan stammered, "I think I can do that, too!"

"What?"

"You know, pick something off the ground."

"It's kind of dangerous." She grinned, lifting her dark thick eyebrows. "I had to practice it all summer before I tried leaning clear to the ground."

"Well, I learn quick," Nathan bragged.

"I'm impressed! Are you really going to try it?" she coaxed, holding onto his left arm with both hands.

"Of course . . . watch this!"

Nathan tossed his hat, brim down, on the dirt.

"Put it the other way," she cautioned.

"I'll do it the hard way," he joshed. Then he rode Onepenny out of the yard.

He whispered to the horse, "You see, I'll ride across, scoop up my hat, wave to Tashawna, and ride on out. Boy, that will really amaze her. I've got a feeling she's one girl that's hard to impress."

When he turned Onepenny around and glanced toward the yard and barn, he could hardly see the hat.

Tashawna waved.

He pulled the stirrup up and laced his hand through it. Nathan thought about what it would be like to lean to the ground while Onepenny galloped through the yard. He could feel a little sweat on his otherwise cold forehead.

Lord . . . eh . . . I sure hope I know what I'm doing.

He didn't.

Nervous about leaning that far out of the saddle, Nathan completely forgot what to do with the reins. Instead of letting them drop to the horn, as Tashawna had, he clutched them tight in his free hand. This brought Onepenny's head around to the left in a sudden jerk towards the barn. The spotted horse, faithful to his master's command, started a collision course towards the gray unpainted barn door.

At the same moment, Nathan was fully extended on the right side of the horse with the upper part of his body halfway to the ground.

I'm going down! I can't stop!

Unfortunately for Nathan, he did stop.

Momentarily.

His left hand, stuck in the stirrup, fastened Nathan to the speeding horse. He could feel himself being dragged back toward Onepenny's rear hooves.

He could hear Tashawna's scream.

He could hear his own.

"Lord, help me!"

The spotted horse had no intention of injuring himself. He whipped around as he neared the barn, propelling Nathan away from the horse, free of the entwining stirrup and the threatening hooves.

Nathan thought he heard Tashawna scream again, but it was a distant sound.

He thought maybe there was an explosion or a crash . . . some vibration against his eardrums. But it quickly disappeared.

Then he thought of nothing at all.

■

It was a complicated dream.

Tashawna was in Galena. She wore a bright red dress with a matching ribbon in her hair and was riding the fast black horse. But Leah, with mud on her face, roped Tashawna off the horse and was screaming, "He ain't my boyfriend!" Nathan ran to help Tashawna to her feet, but Temple Cholach had called him out for a gunfight. Tona was barking his head off while tied in a sack on the back of Onepenny. Nathan desperately wanted his parents to come out and help him, but then he remembered that they had moved to Carson City.

"Nathan? Are you better now?"

He blinked open his eyes and stared up at the underside of the barn roof. Tiny sprinkles of light peeked through the shingles. He tried to move his hands, but they seemed heavy. The back of his head throbbed.

"Nathan?"

It was a soft, sweet voice. It reminded him of a church choir on Easter Sunday morning.

"Tashawna? Onepenny?"

"You crashed into the barn."

He felt something cool on his forehead. Through his blurred vision, Tashawna's smile came into view. There was a wet rag in her hand.

"How's Onepenny?" Nathan muttered.

"Oh, he's fine . . . do you like my necklace?" She beamed.

"Necklace? Your father? He's here? You're the young lady I bought it for?"

"Yes, and he said you have a very good taste in horses and silver jewelry. But he said I had poor taste in boys."

Nathan started to rise to his elbows and then tumbled back down on the dirt.

"My hands . . . a chain? What?"

"Oh, it's just temporary. Daddy said he needed to make sure you didn't run off and turn him in to the law just yet."

Nathan finally understood his incapacity had to do with his hands being shackled around a rough wooden post in the middle of the barn.

"Then . . . you know about the robbery?"

"Daddy told us all about it. It sounded very exciting. We're moving to Carson City, and we're going to buy a great big two-story house, and I get a bed with pink ruffles!"

"He stole that money from the mining company!"

The smile dropped off her face, and she put her hands on her hips. "Well, a mining company took our property. So we're just getting even."

Nathan reached up to wipe his mouth, but the chain snapped his hand back to the splintery post.

"Stealing is wrong!" Nathan protested.

"Says who?"

"The law."

"Ain't no law out here."

"My father's the marshal in Galena!" Nathan insisted.

"He isn't marshal out here." She crossed her arms and shook her head as she talked. "So it's not wrong!"

"But . . . it's always wrong. God says so!"

Tashawna twisted the bear claw on her silver necklace as she spoke. "Well, God ain't out here neither."

"He is too!"

"He is what?" boomed the deep voice of Temple Cholach.

"Daddy, Nathan's come around! But he's talkin' kind of peculiar." Tashawna stood and stepped toward her father.

"You run to the kitchen and bring this boy a plate of food. We don't want him to get hungry."

Nathan stared in fear at the .44 revolver on Cholach's hip as Tashawna disappeared.

"Well, Nathan, I believe we need a man-to-man talk."

"Eh . . . what about?" Nathan croaked.

"Now, I know you didn't accidentally let Onepenny wander all the way from Galena. You were out here looking for me, weren't ya?"

"Eh . . . well." Nathan wished he could stand up. Cholach looked a hundred feet tall from the dirt floor of the barn. "I just went out to Skeeter's. It was Onepenny who broke away and led me here."

"And just why were you looking for me?"

"You know why."

"Because I led you on a wild goose chase up to that cabin?"

"Yeah, that. And the fact that you stole $20,000 from the Shiloh stage, left a man shot, and tricked me into giving you a fresh horse."

Cholach stared at Nathan for a long time.

"Well, you got some of it figured . . . but I didn't trick you into trading horses. That was your idea. And I never fired a shot, let alone shoot a man. He pulled his gun too quick and shot himself in the leg."

Cholach squatted down on his haunches and scratched his head. "Who knows you are out here? Is your daddy going to be looking for me?"

"My daddy and Tick Hill and Deputy Haley and a whole posse will come looking for me!"

"Now that seems strange—so many men looking for a lost boy. Do they know you're in trouble?"

"Eh . . . I sent my friend Leah back to get Dad and the others. They'll be along anytime now."

"Well, they'll have to hurry. We'll be leavin' here real soon."

Cholach left Nathan shackled to the post and proceeded to hitch the draft horses to a wagon located at the north end of the barn.

After a moment, Nathan called out, "You going to take Onepenny?"

Cholach blazed down at Nathan. "I don't steal horses! He belongs to you."

"You going to leave me chained to this post?"

"Yep. But don't worry. Your daddy can free you when he gets here . . . right?"

Nathan cleared his throat. "Are you Colt Blueman?"

"What?" Cholach coughed. "Where did you hear that?"

"Folks around Galena said that you are really Colt Blueman."

"Well, I'm not Blueman, or Hickock, or John Wesley Hardin. I'm just a guy who's trying to get his family through a hard winter."

"By taking other people's money."

"You're young. You wouldn't understand."

"Try me," Nathan offered.

"You've met my wife and my daughter—two of the prettiest and sweetest women in the state of Nevada. They deserve something better than starving to death on this isolated little ranch. We've scratched here for five years, and each year is worse than the one before. The cattle died. Indians stole the horses. The ladies counted on things getting better—that next year we'll make it . . . that all of this will be worthwhile. Well, this is the next year we've waited for, and we don't have enough to last 'til spring."

"So you went out and robbed a stage."

"Look, Nathan, it's done, and now I'll live with the consequences."

"They'll catch you."

"Maybe . . . but if they do, my family will still have their home. I'll purchase it in my wife's name. They can't take it away from her."

"You're willing to go to prison for that?"

"If I have to."

"How do I know this is all true? How do I know you aren't Blueman? How do I know you're really going to buy a house in Carson City? How do I know you aren't some vicious killer?" Nathan blurted out.

"You don't." Cholach offered a slight grin and then pointed his finger at Nathan. "But here's somethin' you can bank on—we're not going to Carson City."

"But you promised Tashawna and your wife!"

"I promised them a home, and I'll get it for them, but not in Carson City."

"Where will you go?"

"That's what the U.S. Marshal's office will spend the next twenty years trying to learn."

"They'll find you," Nathan insisted. "And if they don't, God will judge you."

"I'm sure He will."

Cholach started to lead the team out of the barn.

Nathan called out, "How come you're just now getting here? You robbed the stage last week."

"I spent six days laying a trail out to the white desert of Utah Territory, only to have you follow Onepenny straight to my door. I hadn't counted on you two takin' up the chase."

Cholach and the wagon rattled toward the house, and Nathan strained to see them disappear out the door. Suddenly, Tashawna burst through carrying a plate of food.

"Daddy said it wasn't safe to let you loose, so I guess I'll have to feed you." She grinned.

Nathan struggled to prop himself up on one elbow. "How can you be so happy, knowing your father robbed a stage?"

"Maybe you don't know what it's like bein' poor."

"But when you break God's laws you—"

"You going to preach at me or eat? I don't want to hear about God no more."

"You have to hear it some—" The aroma of hot gravy stopped him in mid-sentence. "Eh . . . I'd like to eat, actually."

Tashawna came to his side and knelt down. Nathan thought he smelled something sweet.

"Have you been eatin' peppermints?"

"No," she said giggling, "it's perfume!"

For a minute he wanted to reach out and put his arm on her shoulder. But his hands were chained to the post.

"Now which do you want first? Bread or stew?" she asked.

Three sharp barks interrupted his answer.

"Tona?" Nathan gasped.

Then a horse with bundled rider limped through the barn doors.

"Leah! What are you doing here?"

"Well, obviously," Leah huffed, "I didn't come to rescue you!"

Tashawna pulled her arm away from Nathan's head.

"What do you mean by that?" she demanded.

"Oh, don't mind me. He surely ain't my boyfriend!" Leah insisted.

8

*L*eah, you're supposed to be in Galena!" Nathan blurted out.

"Well now, you sure don't seem very happy to see me. What are you two doing in the dirt—wrestlin'?"

"So this is Leah?" Tashawna frowned. "No wonder she's not your girlfriend!"

Leah slid off her horse and led the buckskin mare over to the middle of the barn. "Now just what's that suppose to mean?" She pulled off her knit hat and sneered at Tashawna.

Nathan struggled to sit up, but slipped back down on the dirt. "Is there a posse with you? Where's Dad? How did you catch up with me so soon?"

"Well, there ain't no posse. I, eh . . . didn't make it to town."

"What?"

"It was that dog of yours! He pitched such a fit, I put him down a couple miles out of town, and he just spun around and hauled off after you. I've been chasing him for almost two days!" She looked at Nathan but refused to look at Tashawna. "Nathan, what kind of game are you two playin'? What's those chains on your hands for?"

"Leah, get on your horse and get out of here. Cholach's going to—"

"Cholach?" Leah gasped.

The loud banging of the barn door startled all of them.

"Well, if it isn't Nathan's lady friend," Temple Cholach boomed.

"I ain't—" she started to protest.

"Run, Leah! Get out of here!" Nathan shouted.

"Now just where is she going to run to? Too bad about her not making it back to town. I guess Miss Leah is all the help you're going to get." He leered.

Suddenly, Leah sprinted for the ladder to the hay loft. Tashawna started to dash after her, but Nathan caught hold of her wrist with his hand and jerked her back down.

"Daddy!" Tashawna called, "I would have chased her, but Nathan wants me to stay by his side."

"He don't neither," Leah screamed from the rafters. "He jist done that to protect me!"

"Don't worry about her." Cholach nodded. "Where is she going to go? She's too smart to try running back to Galena in the midst of a storm rolling in. There isn't another place for thirty miles. She'll have to come down."

"We just going to leave her there?" Tashawna asked.

"Yep," he said. "But I will take these two horses over and tie them to the rail in front of the house. I wouldn't want her trying to ride off on this lame pony."

"You said you wouldn't take Onepenny!" Nathan protested.

Temple Cholach glared back. He was the closest to being angry Nathan had ever seen him. He pointed his finger at Nathan's face. "I told you once, and I will not tell you again—I do not steal horses! When we leave, I guarantee you that spotted horse will be at your side." Then he turned to his daughter. "Tash, you hurry up and feed him. Then come in to help your mother pack."

Tashawna kept an eye on the loft and began to feed Nathan bites of stew.

"Hoomth ratm goo."

"What did you say?" Tashawna giggled.

Nathan hurriedly swallowed a big piece of meat. "I said, 'This gravy is really good!'"

"Yeah, I made it myself. My mama's taught me everything!"

"Did your mama teach you how to keep your nose turned up like that, or did you learn it all on your own?" Leah shouted.

Tashawna glared up at Leah and then returned to feeding Nathan. "There must be very few girls in Galena if this is the one you like," she muttered.

"I heard that! I can tell you one thing," Leah called out, "I ain't never had to chain a boy to no post in order to get him to talk to me. Did your mama teach you that, too?"

"Honestly, Nathan, your little friend is such a pest!"

"Oh, yeah? Well, bring your curly little pinhead up here and say that!"

"Wait a minute, you two—" Nathan tried to assert.

"Come on down here if you're so brave!" Tashawna left the plate of food on Nathan's lap and stood up.

"I ain't afraid of you," Leah hollered.

"That just shows how dumb you are!"

"I ain't dumb. I can read . . . can't I, Nathan?"

"Yes, she—"

"So what? Everyone can read!" Tashawna screamed back. "I see you're still in the loft. What's the matter? You afraid to climb down the ladder?"

"I surely ain't afraid of the likes of you. Nathan, you want me to beat her up or should I hightail it for Galena?"

"Neither!" Nathan called. "I don't want either of you getting hurt!"

"I certainly won't get hurt," Tashawna boasted.

"I'm going to whip her, Nathan. I swear, I'm going to whip her!" Leah boasted.

Nathan was still chewing stew when Leah climbed down the ladder and jumped the last three steps to the dirt floor.

"No, Leah, wait!"

Tashawna dove at Leah as her feet hit the ground, and Nathan stared as both girls slapped, scratched, and yanked at each other's hair.

"Don't!" he yelled.

Tona ran inside the barn and began frantically barking at the tumbling pair. After rolling intertwined across the dirt, Leah sprang to her feet and slammed her doubled-up fist into Tashawna's face. Nathan figured that it must have hit her nose because he could see blood starting to trickle across her upper lip and drip into her mouth.

Tashawna smeared the blood across the back of her hand and ducked another wild swing. She staggered back, and Leah dove for her legs.

This time Tashawna delivered the damaging blow by kicking Leah in the side of her head. The lace-up boot caught Leah just under her right eye, and she rolled over clutching her face, trying not to be kicked again.

Neither girl cried.

"Cholach!" Nathan screamed. "Cholach, get in here. They'll kill each other! Cholach!"

Amidst the shouts, screams, and constant barking, Temple Cholach swooped down from out of nowhere and picked up Leah around the waist. As she fought and kicked, he plopped her to the dirt by another post and quickly tied her hands behind it. Then, grabbing an empty oat sack, he tied her feet securely.

"Tashawna, get into the house and get cleaned up," he commanded. "You two sure are a lot of trouble." He looked at Nathan and Leah.

"Missy, you going to be all right?" he asked.

"I ain't Missy, and I'm fine. There's nothin' she could do to hurt me!"

"Maybe not," said Cholach with a shrug, "but you'll have a big shiner on that eye come morning."

"A shiner? She gave me a black eye?"

"Now you two just behave yourselves, and I'll bring those horses back before we leave. My word, that dog barks a lot!"

"Mr. Cholach?" Nathan called. "I think Leah should get something to eat, too."

"Yeah. I'll take care of it." He turned to leave the barn, and Tona followed him out.

Nathan lay still until Cholach was completely out of sight.

"Leah?"

"Yeah?"

"Are you really all right?"

"Just some scratches."

"How's your eye?"

"It hurts."

"How come you fought her?"

"'Cause she was makin' fun of me."

"And you were makin' fun of her."

"She shouldn't have said those things."

Neither spoke for a few minutes.

"I thought maybe you two could become friends." Nathan broke the silence. "You really have a lot in common."

"Like what?"

"Well, you both . . . you know . . . like the outdoors, and you don't mind speakin' up, and neither one of you is bashful, and you like green dresses . . . and, well you both are very pretty girls."

"There ain't nothin' alike in us—" Leah began her protest, then stopped mid-sentence.

"Nathan . . . you ain't just sayin' that 'cause I got a black eye, are you?"

"What?"

"About me being pretty."

"No, I meant it."

"You ain't never told me that before. Nobody ever told me that before."

"Not even your father?"

"Daddys don't count."

He could see that Leah was staring at the ground.

"Nathan, are you mad at me?"

"What about?"

"You know . . . lettin' Tona get loose and comin' back here without seeing your daddy first?"

"No, I'm not mad. It's my own stupid fault. I don't know why I rode out here. We both ought to be back in Galena. This is dumb."

"Kind of like you and me and Colin in that cabin with Devere, ain't it?"

"Worse. We couldn't help it that time, but here—we don't even have to be here!"

"What are we going to do?" she asked.

"We'll ride home after they leave."

"You really think they'll turn us loose?"

"Yep."

"But that Cholach's a stage robber!"

"I know," Nathan added, "but I just don't think he's made a habit of doing bad things."

For a few more moments they said nothing. He could see Leah tug at her bonds. He had given up doing the same to his. As the barn got darker, he could tell it was either getting late in the day or heavy with storm clouds.

Lord, all I want is my horse . . . and Leah's horse and for us to go home. Someone ought to be out here chasing robbers, but not me and Leah. I don't know why good people like Cholach take to doing wrong. I don't know why sometimes I do wrong. Now I know You're probably disgusted about how I keep getting into these jams. I just don't have a lot of common sense, but I could learn, Lord.

"Nathan . . . do you like her?" Leah spoke quietly.

"Tashawna?"

"Is that her name? It ain't a Bible name. Anyway, do you like her?"

"You ought to see her ride Onepenny. She can do tricks you wouldn't believe."

"Yeah . . . but do you like her?"

"She can jump a fence while hunkered down to one side ridin' Indian!"

"Nathan . . . do you like her?"

"I think she's real nice."

"Nathan T. Riggins, I'm askin' you if she's your girlfriend!"

"Ah . . . I . . . I'm not saying if I have a girlfriend, and I'm not saying if I don't!" he muttered.

"That's right—just don't go forgettin' it," she huffed.

Tashawna and her father came into the barn. She was carrying another plate of food. Nathan could see that she had cleaned her face, and there was no trace of the earlier fight.

"Young lady," Cholach addressed his daughter, "do what

your mother told you. And when you're through, come on back to the house. We're almost ready to leave." He turned and went out the door.

Tashawna cleared her throat and stood on one foot and then the other. "Mama says that I need to apologize for not acting like a lady. She said that I should tell you that my behavior was unbecoming, and she said I had to say I'm sorry and . . . you know, ask you to forgive me." Tashawna let out a big sigh when she had completed her speech.

Leah gazed at her for a moment.

"Do you forgive her, Leah?" Nathan demanded.

Leah looked up, squinting through her black eye. "Do you always do what your mama tells you?"

"Yes," Tashawna said with a nod, "don't you?"

"I ain't got no mama, and my daddy's new wife don't tell me nothin' but clean my feet and do the chores."

"Leah?" Nathan pressed.

"Okay . . . I guess I have to forgive you."

"Good, now I'll feed you some dinner," Tashawna offered.

"Untie me. I'll eat my own dinner. These ropes is pinchin' my wrists."

"I can't. Daddy says to leave you both tied. Now come on, Cupcake, open up and you can taste how good my gravy really is."

"You ain't feedin' me nothin'!" Leah protested.

"Come on, Leah." Nathan called. "You got to have something to eat."

"She ain't feedin' me." Leah squirmed causing a piece of stew to hit her cheek instead of her mouth and slide down into her lap.

"My, your little friend is sloppy, Nathan. Aren't you, dear?" Tashawna drawled.

"Don't 'dear' me. Untie me and I'll pull every one of those lovely curls out of your head and stuff them in your—"

Tashawna jammed a big piece of stew into Leah's mouth. Leah instantly spit it out, hitting Tashawna in the neck, who countered by dumping the entire plate on Leah's head.

Leah's scream caused Temple Cholach to sprint through the barn door.

"She's a witch!" Leah sobbed.

"She spit all over me like a goat!" Tashawna cried. "I'm going in the house!"

She ran out of the barn, and Cholach went over and lit a lantern. "Sorry, Miss Leah, Tashawna shouldn't have done that. Sometimes raising a daughter is a mighty difficult thing."

"Especially if she doesn't have a good example to follow!" Nathan blurted out.

I'm dead! Why did I say that, Lord?

"Son, I don't expect you to agree, but out here things is wild. Right and wrong becomes all blurred. Sometimes a man just has to do what's best for his family."

"But it's just plain wrong! Stealin' is wrong."

Cholach hung the lantern on a peg near Nathan and sat down on a bench near the wall of the barn. "Did you see that ridge up there to the north when you rode in?"

"Yeah."

"Well, I used to own the land clear up to there. It takes about that much land to make a livin' running a cow and calf outfit out here."

"What happened to it?"

"The politicians redrew the county line, claimed that it was now in Elko County and belonged to some mining corporation in San Francisco. That ain't right. But like I said, it's all fuzzy out here."

"It's not fuzzy to God."

"No, I reckon it ain't. And like I told you before, I'll cross that bridge when I come to it."

Then he pulled an extra harness off the wall and began to leave the barn carrying the lantern.

"Mr. Cholach?" Nathan called out. "Can I talk to Tashawna before you all leave?" Then looking at Leah and back at Cholach, he added, "You know . . . alone?"

"I'll see what I can figure out." Cholach nodded and left the barn.

"What do you want to talk to her for? She don't care about us. She's just playin' with you like a cat with a mouse. Can't you see that? Nathan, sometimes boys can act so dumb! Just 'cause she's got curls, it don't mean—"

Temple Cholach reentered the barn and scooped up Tona, plopping him in an enclosed stall. The gray and white dog began to howl.

"Now it's time to make a few adjustments here," Cholach added. He reached down with a wrench and loosed Nathan's shackles. Then holding onto the chain with his hand, he led Nathan out of the barn.

"Where you goin'?" Leah called.

"He'll be back, Miss Leah."

Nathan staggered across the yard, his legs stiff from an afternoon of inactivity. A few flakes of snow brushed against his face, melted, then puddled in the dirt on his cheek.

Tashawna was waiting inside a small shed. "This is my blacksmith shop," Cholach explained, "but the fire's not hot enough, so I'm going to chain you to this anvil. You and Tashawna can talk for a minute. I'll be right back after I board up the windows of the house."

"It's going to be dark soon." She nodded her head towards the storm clouds.

"Are you going to move everything?" Nathan asked.

"No, we're going to buy all new things!" She smiled.

"With stolen money?"

"I don't care. I'm glad he did it," she proclaimed.

"You are?"

"Yes, he said we'll pay that mining company back if we can. In the meantime we can have a chance to get a fresh start in Carson City."

"He won't pay it back, and you aren't going to Carson City," Nathan blurted out.

"We are too! Daddy said—"

"He wouldn't let me know where you are going. That's just a decoy. He knows I'll tell the law."

"Are you going to turn my daddy in to the sheriff?"

"I don't have any choice."

"Sure you do. You could just ride home and forget it."

"I can't do that! It's wrong to steal. If you let people break some laws, soon they'll break all laws. Then you got nothing but a fight every day of your life."

"Well, it don't matter. We'll be way far away before you ever get back to Galena."

"Tashawna," Nathan spoke softly, "did you ever wish we could have met some other place? You know, what if you would have moved to Galena and just lived down the street?"

"Yeah . . . but I haven't ever lived down the street from anyone. Don't you see? That's what makes this move so exciting. A house, and a yard, and neighbors—on a real street in a real town!"

"Well, I wish I could be happy for you, Tashawna. I surely wish I could."

"Why don't you come visit me?"

"What?"

"You know . . . we'll get all settled in our new place, and then maybe you could ride the train and come visit me. We'll walk down a big wide street, and there'll be trollies and street lamps and ladies with fancy hats. Do you think I'd look good in a fancy hat?"

"I'd imagine you'd look nice . . . eh," Nathan stammered, "in just about anything."

"You two about through?" Cholach interrupted.

"Daddy! He was just gettin' to the sweet-talkin' part!"

"Well, it's a good thing I showed up," he said laughing. "Nathan, I want to be straight up with you. I like you. So does Tashawna. I know you've got to do what you've got to do. And I'm the same way. If our paths ever should cross . . . well, I hope we can be friends, and I do hope you'll come visit Tashawna. Now, girl, bring that spotted pony around here."

He began to bend a metal strap in the hot coals. Nathan heard it pop and sizzle as Cholach plunged it into a pail of cold water.

"What are you going to do?" Nathan asked.

"Well, I'm going to slow you down a bit."

"You going to hobble Onepenny with those chains?"

"I'm going to hobble you both."

"What do you mean?" Nathan tried to back away, but couldn't.

In a matter of seconds, Cholach had a shackle fastened to Nathan's right leg and the other to Onepenny's left pastern. About two foot of chain dangled in between.

"Now, you can walk Onepenny back to Galena, but you won't ride him."

"I could get hurt. What if he bolts!"

"He won't. Onepenny's a fine horse. You can always trust a spotted horse," Cholach offered.

"But you can't always trust people!" Nathan complained.

"That's true . . . very true."

9

*F*or several minutes Nathan stood watching the wagon roll out of sight. The snowflakes no longer swirled about him, but rather raged in from the northwest. He buttoned up his coat and pulled his hat low. Nathan felt cold and very alone.

But not for long.

"Nathan! What's going on out there?" Leah's screaming voice could barely be heard above the howl of the storm.

"Leah, can you hear me?" Nathan shouted.

"Come in the barn! Come untie me!"

"I can't . . . Cholach hobbled me to Onepenny?"

"What? I didn't hear you!" she screamed.

I've got to get to the barn! Lord, help me!

"Nathan!"

He ignored Leah's cries.

"Look, Onepenny, I don't know how to do this . . . why don't we take a small step towards the barn, okay?"

Nathan stepped to the end of the chain, tugged at Onepenny, and then fell on his face. Sharp frozen ruts of the yard thrust through the thin layer of snow and cut his cheek. His ankle throbbed.

"We got to get out of the storm!" he shouted at the horse. He stood up and coaxed Onepenny again.

"Listen . . . lift your left foot and step out . . . " Nathan lifted the spotted horse's hoof and pulled it forward.

"That's the way . . . now let's do it again."

This time just as Nathan had the chain extended, Onepenny jerked his left foot up underneath himself, which flipped Nathan's right foot backwards. Again he dove headfirst into the snow-covered, frozen Nevada dirt.

"Nathan, don't go off and leave me! Nathan!" Leah cried.

"Quit yellin' at me!" he hollered. "I'll be there as quick as I can!"

Once again he tried to coax the spotted horse forward. This time when he began to fall, Nathan reached out and grabbed Onepenny's neck, clenching both hands around it. This caused him to swing under the horse's shoulders with his feet now dragging between Onepenny's front hooves.

If I let go, he'll trample me!

Nathan didn't let go.

His interlocked fingers ached.

His face was buried in the long winter hair on Onepenny's breast.

His right ankle took a thrashing every time the horse staggered forward.

But Nathan held on.

"Call Onepenny," he turned his head and screamed at Leah. "Call him!"

"Onepenny! Come here, boy . . . come here!" Leah bellowed from inside the barn.

Slowly the horse limped toward the barn with the burden of Nathan's body hanging to his neck.

"Nathan," Leah cried out as they finally entered the barn, "did he kick you?"

"Keep calling him! I've got to get close enough to untie you!"

"Thataboy . . . come on, Onepenny . . . good boy!" she urged.

"Whoa, boy, whoa!" Nathan called, then collapsed on the dirt in front of the horse. He lay on his back staring up as the horse glanced expressionlessly at him and then at Leah.

Regaining his breath, Nathan scampered out from under Onepenny but remained on his hands and knees. He fumbled at the rope on her wrists.

"Come on . . . come on!" he mumbled to himself.

Finally the ropes fell free. Leah rubbed her hands and untied her feet. Then she stood up and stretched her legs.

"Are you hurt?" she asked.

"My ankle aches, my face is a little cut, and I'm out of breath . . . but I'll live. I'm sure not going to try it that way again!"

Leah took a burlap sack and tried to wipe the stew off her head and shoulders.

"What are we going to do?" she asked.

"Let's go home," Nathan suggested.

"Tonight?"

"Whenever I figure out how to walk with this horse!"

Nathan stood up with his hand on Onepenny's shoulder. "Leah, I think you'll find a lantern on the far wall of the loft. See if it still has any fuel. Bring it over here and we'll light it. Then close the barn door and let Tona out of the stall. I don't want him running off after Cholach."

"Nathan, how are you going to get that chain off?"

"Take it to the blacksmith in Galena, I guess. Cholach took his blacksmithing tools."

"But what if you cain't ride? How are you going to get home?"

107

"Walk."

Leah reached up and rubbed Onepenny's cheeks. "You cain't walk like that. Why, if this horse breaks out, he'll drag you through the rocks or kick you to death."

"Yeah . . . I've thought about that, but I don't have any choice."

"Are we really leaving tonight?" Leah finally asked.

"I don't know." Nathan sighed. "I've got to figure this out. You didn't get much supper. Do you want some of my jerky?" He dug in his saddlebag.

"Yeah . . . thanks!"

For several moments they chewed on the dried meat. Nathan could feel the cold wind of the storm seeping through the cracks in the barn.

"Nathan . . . I don't think that Tashawna's very nice. She poked fun at me, dumped food on me, and tried to make me feel dumb. Well, that ain't right. I ain't stupid and I ain't ugly. She just lives on a dirt poor ranch. I can be as uppity as she can! How come she has to act that way?"

"I don't know, Leah." Nathan motioned by nodding his head. "I'm sorry you had to get mixed up in this. If you would have stayed home like I told you—"

"Well, I didn't, so just shut yourself up," she insisted. "Anyway, I'm cold. Can we build a fire or something?"

"You can't build a fire in a barn," he cautioned. "Pull my bedroll off my saddle. You can wrap up in my blankets."

She grabbed the bedroll. "It's soaking wet! What did you do, sleep in a creek?"

"Oh . . . great . . . well, maybe we ought to build a fire. You know, just a little one."

Within moments a small fire was blazing. The smoke drifted slowly and began to fill the barn. Leah stretched out

Nathan's blankets to dry and then sat on the ground leaning against his saddle.

"I think I'll sleep a little while right here. Wake me up when you're ready to go."

"I'll try to get some sleep next to Onepenny, but first I'm going to try to walk him around the inside of the barn. I've got to figure out how to make this work."

Warmed up and out of chill of the storm, Nathan stood up beside the horse. "Onepenny, I know you don't like this, and I don't like it either. But we're kind of stuck with each other for a while, so we might as well do the best we can."

Nathan left his right hand on Onepenny's shoulder. Even through the long hair, he could feel the horse's strong muscles. Then he applied some pressure with his hand and tried to move his foot and Onepenny's foot forward.

"Come on, boy! When you feel the pressure, take one small step."

The first attempt was awkward, but by the fourth try, everything went a little smoother. The fifth time was perfect.

"Thataboy! You did it!" Nathan rubbed Onepenny's muzzle, cheek, and neck. "Come on, let's try it some more!"

Slowly around and around the barn they went—horse . . . boy . . . and dog. Tona insisted on walking at their pace on the left side of Nathan. Both Nathan and Onepenny favored their chained leg and limped as they walked, but soon they developed a rhythm and seldom missed a step.

When they did get off on their timing, it was Nathan who fell down. He finally walked Onepenny over near his stall, fed him some oats, and then came back towards the fire.

"Onepenny, I hope you don't have any nightmares!"

The spotted horse blinked his eyes slowly and gazed at the flickering flames. Tona, who seldom spent a night indoors, made a path between sleeping next to Nathan and checking the barn door to see if it had opened.

■

Daylight came dimly, slowly. Heavy clouds almost touched the ground as Nathan and Leah saddled their horses.

"It ain't snowing right now, but there's three inches of fresh stuff on the ground," she reported. "The house is boarded up all around, and there ain't no tracks anywhere!"

"Well . . . we're ready to leave," Nathan announced. "Take one of my bedroll blankets. That blue one looks dry. Wrap it around your head and let it fall over your coat. It will feel a lot colder when we get out into that wind. You can't ride your horse. She's lame. You did enough damage pushing her yesterday," Nathan scolded.

"I know. I'll walk her," Leah offered.

"No, I need you up on Onepenny. You might be able to see further. You have to lead her from up there."

"What will I be looking for?" she asked as she yanked herself up into the saddle.

"A short cut."

"What short cut?"

Nathan coached Onepenny, and they walked along in unison out of the barn. "We should be able to cut straight west and hit the Galena to Austin road. That way we might be able to get home late tonight. If we go way north to Skeeter's cabin, it will take us two days."

"But how do you know there's a shortcut?"

"There has to be one somewhere. Tashawna mentioned once that her father could push Onepenny and make it in a long day."

Leah's eyes sparked. "You two got real chummy now, didn't you? Besides, with you limping along, we can't make it back in a day."

"It might be a very long day," Nathan added. "But we're getting home by tonight!"

Nathan was bundled inside a tightly buttoned coat with the collar turned high. His wide-brimmed hat was tied on with the stampede string pulling the side brims over his ears. Except when cuing the horse, he kept his hands jammed in his pockets, his eyes squinted into the cold wind, and his slightly chapped lips pinched tight.

Within only a few yards of the barn, they established a pattern that set the pace for their entire journey. Tona led, but stayed only a step or two straight in front of Nathan, constantly turning around to seek direction. Then came Nathan and Onepenny. The spotted horse held his head high and ears forward, even though the cold wind was blowing into their faces. Nathan had set the bit and bridle, but he allowed the reins to drape over Onepenny's mane and loop the saddle horn.

The two-foot chain linking Nathan and the horse served as the only lead "rope" needed. Nathan limped along in unison with the spotted horse. He found he only needed to touch Onepenny for a few steps each time they started up to get the timing right. After that, the horse seemed to know just how big a stride Nathan could take in the snow.

Aboard Onepenny, Leah found she could wrap the blanket over her head in such a way that only a small slit exposed her eyes. Through that she peered out into the gray and white sameness of the rolling landscape ahead of them.

She held the leads to the mare, who trailed along, head down. At that slow pace, Nathan could hardly notice the horse's limp. They talked very little except to discuss directions.

"I think that's the route up to Skeeter's cabin." Leah pointed north.

"I think you're right . . . look at Tona. He wants to go back north. It's the only way he's made the trip, which means west should be straight for that rise."

"That rise? There's a rise in every direction! Nathan," Leah said from under the blanket, "my legs are cold."

"How did you make it out here yesterday?"

"I was ridin' fast, and the mare's flanks were warm."

"Maybe you can fold your legs under you on the saddle. That way they'll be covered by the blanket."

"Oh, sure, and how am I suppose to keep from fallin' off?"

Nathan shrugged his shoulders and raised both arms. "Yeah . . . you're probably right. I saw Tashawna do it, but she's an incredible rider—"

"Ta-shaw-na," Leah mimicked. "Where did she ever get a name like that? I bet she made it up herself."

Within seconds Leah had pulled her legs up under the blanket. "It's no big deal, really. She ain't the only one that can do it!"

They traveled several more miles before she spoke again. "Should we build a fire and warm up?"

"Nope. We've got to push on. We'll stop at noon."

"How do we know when noon is?"

"Noon is when me and Onepenny get tired of dragging this chain!" Nathan announced. The day hardly lightened at all, and the jangle of the chain could barely be heard above the steady whistle of the wind.

Somewhere in the December snows of Nevada, on the southern slope of the Shoshone Range—with no other human, animal, or man-made structure in sight—they stopped to build a scraggly little fire and ate the last two pieces of jerky.

"We need more wood on the fire!" Leah complained.

Nathan bent his face close to the flames, but the warmth of the fire didn't penetrate his cold cheeks.

"There isn't any more wood. A few scraps of dead sage—that's about it. We need to move on anyway," Nathan reminded her.

"Are you sure we can make it in one day?"

"If we don't quit," Nathan assured her. "The Galena road is that way, and we have to cross it sooner or later."

■

The afternoon light had blended into the gray, stormy stillness of twilight when Tona left his usual place and ran off to the north, barking wildly.

"Tona! Come back!" Leah yelled.

"What is it?" Nathan asked her. "What does he see?"

"I cain't see anything! 'Course my one eye is nearly swole shut."

"Tona won't bark at the wind! Maybe someone's come out to rescue us!"

"I cain't see anything! It's getting dark and those clouds are so . . . hey! There it is. Do you see it?"

"What is it?" Nathan called again.

"It's a . . . a horse . . . a cow covered with snow . . . a big cow!"

"Tona!" Nathan yelled. "Come here!"

"There it is!" Leah hollered. "Maybe it's a bull."

"It's a buffalo!" Nathan moaned. "Oh . . . man . . . Tona! Tona! Get over here!"

"It can't be a buffalo. There ain't any buffalo left in Nevada!"

"Well, I don't know what it's doing here, but it's a buffalo!"

"He looks mad!" Leah yelled. "He's going to charge at Tona!"

"Tona! Get over here!" Nathan screamed. "Leah, get off Onepenny. Quick!"

He almost yanked her to the ground.

"Take the mare and run back down the slope. He's going to charge the—"

Tona barked.

Leah ran.

Nathan howled.

The buffalo began to charge the horses.

Nathan could hear himself screaming, "No! Onepenny! No! Stand your ground! Please don't run! Please!"

He grabbed the horse around the neck and held tight, almost swinging his feet off the ground.

The mare panicked. She reared, jerking the reins from Leah's hand. Then she galloped off to the south, never slowing.

Onepenny whinnied, snorted, turned his rear end toward the buffalo and kicked his back feet wildly. His front feet stayed in place.

Lord, I'm going to be trampled to death. I don't want to die! Help!

The snow-covered, shaggy buffalo pulled up instantly at the sight of flying hooves. It turned and trotted to the east about fifty feet, then spun around, and faced them.

Once again it was still—like a statue in a park—waiting for them to make the first move.

"Leah, are you hurt?"

"I think my hand got burned by the reins," she reported.

"Quick! Grab Tona!" he shouted.

Leah ran from her safe position toward Tona and the buffalo. She scooped up the surprised dog and returned to Nathan.

Onepenny was still snorting. His ears stood straight up, and his head was turned back to watch the buffalo, who now showed no sign of moving.

Leah stuck her face close to Nathan's. "Did you get kicked?"

"No . . . did you see him? Did you see Onepenny? He stood by me! He actually did it!"

"What are you going to do with Tona?" she asked as she clutched the squirming dog and kept one eye on the buffalo.

"Sack him like before," Nathan commanded. "We can't have him stirring up more trouble."

"You think there's more buffalo?" Leah asked.

"Did you ever hear about one being by itself?"

"What about my horse?"

"If she keeps running south, we'll have to let her go. We've got to go west. Maybe she'll slow down, come back and look for us, and then follow Onepenny's trail."

"Climb up there, Leah, and I'll hand you Tona."

"I don't think he likes it in the sack," she commented.

"Nope. I don't reckon he does, but maybe he'll keep your feet warm."

With the coming of darkness, their only light was an eerie faint glow off the snow. The storm raged on, and Nathan pulled his bandanna over his face.

"Shouldn't we stop?" Leah yelled out. "We cain't see anything!"

"We'll be at the Galena Road any minute now. We have to push on."

Suddenly Onepenny halted. Nathan tripped on the taut chain and fell in the snow.

"Hey!"

"What happened?" Leah called.

"He stopped! Come on, Onepenny! Come on, boy, we're just about to the road. Then it will be easier!" Nathan regained his stance and patted the horse.

Once again, tapping the horse's shoulder, Nathan moved his foot forward, but the horse didn't budge. This time Nathan fell to his knees in the snow.

"Maybe he's tired," Leah offered. "I'm tired and hungry and frozen and . . ."

Tona drowned out Leah's complaints.

"Come on, Onepenny . . . keep Tona quiet!" he hollered up at her.

"How do I keep him quiet?"

"Just clamp his jaws shut or something!"

"I ain't puttin' my hand near his jaws," she stated bluntly. "Maybe there's another buffalo out there."

"What?" Nathan yelled above the yapping of the dog.

"A buffalo. Is there another buffalo?" she screamed.

"No. Couldn't be . . . could there? Hand me my matches out of the saddlebag—on the left side."

"What?"

"Give me my matches."

"Well, you don't have to scream!"

Nathan lit a match and held it as far in front of Onepenny as he could reach. When the match struck, Tona stopped barking.

"What do you see?" Leah called.

"Nothin.'"

"How about down there . . . on the ground in front of Onepenny."

"Good grief!" Nathan shouted.

"What is it?"

"Nothing. Absolutely nothing!"

"You can't see anything?"

"Nothing but a hole—a giant hole!" Nathan ranted. "No wonder Onepenny didn't want to go on."

Leah slid out of the saddle and in doing so dropped the sack with Tona into the snow. The dog scampered free.

"Let me see," she insisted.

"It's just a hole. We'll have to circle around, that's all," Nathan advised.

"Toss a match down there. Let's see how deep it is."

Nathan lit another match and tossed it in the hole.

"That ain't no hole!" Leah shouted as they watched the match sail downward. "We're smack dab on top of the Lewis Cliffs!"

"East of town?"

"Yeah."

"How do you know?" Nathan asked.

"'Cause I ran away from home one time and tried to spend the night up here and got scared to death and ran back home before daylight. I stumbled along the edge of these cliffs and purt' near killed myself."

"I never knew that."

"There's a lot of things you don't know about me, Nathan T. Riggins!"

Tona's barking caught their attention.

"He got loose!" Leah shouted.

"That's okay. Maybe he knows his way in from here."

"Well, I ain't walking along the edge of that cliff!"

"Look, we'll keep Onepenny on the cliff side. You either

117

hold onto my hand or to Onepenny's tail. He won't lead us over the cliff; he's proved that."

"I ain't holdin' no horse's tail," she insisted, clutching Nathan's hand tightly.

She didn't release her grip until they entered the town of Galena an hour and a half later.

10

*D*ogs barked.

Oil lanterns flickered.

People scurried in the shadows.

Leah finally released Nathan's hand and climbed up the stairs to her home above the barber shop.

He limped along to the marshal's office, only to find Deputy Haley, who then ran across town to get Nathan's father and the blacksmith. Within an hour Nathan had been freed from his hobble, told his father all about Cholach, gobbled down several bowls of soup, and crawled into his bed, which had never felt so soft and warm before.

He just knew he would instantly fall asleep.

He was wrong.

Lord, this didn't quite go the way I figured it. I mean, I didn't plan on making my folks mad at me for staying out in the storm again. And I didn't plan on Cholach being such a nice family man. And I didn't plan on meeting someone like Tashawna . . .

The thought of Tashawna flying across the yard on the back of Onepenny interrupted his prayer. He remembered the sparkle in her dark eyes, the curls in her hair, her secret kind of smile that made Nathan want to do most anything she asked.

Lord, I know Mr. Cholach needs to pay for his crime. He should be caught and the money returned, and he should go to

jail, but . . . well, I just don't think he's all that bad. Not like
Devere or one of those . . . maybe You could . . . and
Tashawna and Mrs. Cholach—they didn't do anything. I'm
afraid they'll be out in the cold if he gets caught. Lord, they
deserve better than that, I think. I like it better when bad people are really bad. I'm sure glad You can figure this out because
it's too confusing for me.

And Lord, thanks for giving me Onepenny. He stood
right there with me. He always seems to know what I need to
do next. It's like we've known each other all our lives. He just
wouldn't abandon me . . . even though it was all my fault.

Sort of like You . . . isn't he?

Jesus, I'm sure glad You've stuck by me, too. And You
weren't even chained to my leg.

For several minutes he stared at the blackness of his room.

Lord . . . it's me, Nathan, again. Listen, I'm going to
really try not to do so many dumb things. Help me not to
cause my parents so much worry. But I was wonderin' . . . You
know, if I slip up and get in trouble, well, I sure would appre-
ciate it if You would stick by me anyway. Thanks, Lord.

It was well after 10:00 A.M the next morning when
Nathan finally woke up. He scrubbed up his face, arms, and
feet. He pulled on his heaviest wool shirt, slipped on his jacket,
and hurried around to complete his chores. Then he hiked
down to his father's office.

Marshal Riggins sat behind his desk—an old bank door
balanced on two barrels. Deputy Haley and another man were
talking to him, but the conversation ceased as Nathan entered
the room.

"Dad, I thought of something else. I forgot to tell you that
the team was a couple of those big, old long-haired draft horses."

"Thanks, Nate. I'll send that along to the county sheriff."

"Aren't you going after them?"

"Nope. Not enough information. You said they talked about Carson City, but you were sure they weren't headed that way. And they left before the snow fell, so we wouldn't find any tracks."

"He gets to go free?"

"Well," Marshal Riggins replied, "I hope not. The county sheriff will likely as not pick him up. I've always said, no man who breaks God's laws is ever free."

"That's what I told him."

"You told Cholach to settle up with God?"

"More or less."

Mr. Riggins stood and walked Nathan to the door. "Listen, you have a little settling up with God to do yourself, right?"

"You mean about staying out in the storm again and all that?"

"Yep."

"Yeah. I can't believe I did it. It won't happen again."

"Nope. It won't," the marshal agreed. "Your mother and I don't want you to leave town, even for a ride, until after Christmas."

"I can't ride until after—"

"I said you can't ride outside of town. We want a few weeks where we don't have to wait up all night wondering when you'll get home."

"Yes, sir. I'd better go check on Onepenny. I think he got scraped up." He started out the door and then turned to face his father. "Did I tell you how Onepenny can—"

"You told me that spotted horse could do everything but walk on water, and he was practicing that! Now go on." Marshal Riggins shooed him out the door.

Nathan and Tona ambled towards the stables. The clean white snow crunched under his feet, and the sun was bright in a cold blue sky. Just as he stepped out from under a covered sidewalk, a snowball struck the back of his coat.

"Leah Walker!" he hollered. "You get down here!"

Skipping down the wooden stairs along the alley, she called, "How'd ya know it was me?"

"Because Tona didn't bark. He barks at everyone on earth except me and you! Besides," he said laughing, "you're the only one who lives above the barber shop."

"Did ya git in trouble?" she asked.

"Yeah . . . sort of."

"Did ya git a whippin'?"

"No. Did you?"

"Nah, but she cried."

"Your stepmother cried?"

"I guess she sort of worries about me. She don't think I ought to be running around with the likes of you. She said if I expect to be treated like a lady, I'd better start acting like a lady."

They continued to walk to the livery.

"Well, I suppose she's right."

Nathan glanced at Leah. He saw that all the stew had been scrubbed off her head. Her hair hung straight to each side of her freckled face. The black eye was the only blemish he could find.

"You going to start doing that?"

"What?" She looked him in the eyes.

"Acting like a lady?"

"Nah." She grinned.

"Good. Then I'll race you to Onepenny!" Nathan shouted.

Suddenly Leah kicked him in the shin. As he grabbed his leg and hobbled out into the road, she started to sprint to the big barn at the edge of town.

"Hey! That's cheating! You can't do that!" Nathan raced to overtake Leah and Tona who had half a block head start.

She was just rounding the corrals when Nathan caught up to her. He reached out to grab her. Avoiding his tackle, she tripped over Tona who had slowed to watch the action. Nathan ran and touched the barn door and then spun around yelling, "I won! I beat you and you cheated!"

Leah was still lying in the snow trying to catch her breath.

"Maybe . . . maybe," she panted, "maybe I'll give this ladylike stuff a try."

"Hey, you want to watch me ride Onepenny?" Nathan called.

"Eh . . . not really. I think I'll go home," she said softly.

"Leah? Are you all right? I'm sorry if I hurt you."

She rose to her feet, scooping up a handful of snow. "You couldn't hurt me if you tried!" she yelled and slammed a snowball into the barn door just above Nathan's head.

Nathan was surprised to see how little damage was done to Onepenny's pastern. He saddled the horse and led him by the reins out into the street. As they strolled along, he noticed how Onepenny got in step and walked along right beside him, just as they had done when chained together.

"You like that, eh, boy? Okay, let's just see how you do going across town."

Nathan drooped the reins over the saddle horn and meandered towards the Mercantile. Onepenny kept with him, stride for stride.

"Thataboy!" Nathan encouraged. He purposely walked Onepenny by several wagons and horses that were leaving town, down past the string of mounts hitched in front of the Crazy Horse, and right in front of a shouting match rolling out from the lobby of the Humboldt Hotel. Onepenny never flinched. He stuck right by Nathan's side.

Nathan climbed the stair to the wooden sidewalk at the front of the Welsh Miners' Hall, and Onepenny climbed with him, walking across the sidewalk and down the other side.

An old man leaned in the doorway of the hall.

"That horse follows you around like a dog!" he called. "Them spotted horses is mighty fine, mighty fine. Don't you ever git rid of him, ya hear?"

"No, sir. I don't aim to."

The Austin to Battle Mountain Station stage pulled into town and stopped in front of the livery to change horses. Nathan mounted up and rode back across town. Approaching the corrals next to the livery, he decided to impress the passengers. Racing Onepenny to the empty corral, he jumped him over the gate. Then circling inside the corral, he stood in the saddle and tipped his hat to the stage.

"I can do that backwards!" a familiar voice called out from inside the darkened stagecoach.

Nathan leaped over the fence and hurried to look into the stage.

"Tashawna? Mrs. Cholach?"

"Hi, Nathan." Tashawna waved and climbed down out of the stage. Nathan noticed she wore a brand-new long coat and new lace-up shoes, and she carried a small leather satchel.

"Can we . . . talk in private?" she asked.

"Uh . . . sure. How about over by Onepenny? What are you doing here? Where's your father? Where are you going?"

"Look, you were right." She only glanced at him once and then studied Onepenny.

"About what?"

"About some things being right and some being wrong."

"You mean about stealing the money?"

"Yeah."

"Did your father give himself up?"

"No—not yet anyway. Listen, when we left you, we headed to Austin. Daddy admitted we weren't going to Carson City. Like you said, that was all a lie to throw you off our trail. He said we were going to Texas—that he had friends there."

"And then Mama started crying, saying she'd rather scratch it out on the ranch than be on the run. And I guess I started crying, too."

"What happened then?" Nathan asked.

"Daddy said it was all your fault."

Nathan's mouth dropped open. "My fault? What did I do?"

"I guess when you said God would judge us, it sort of reminded my mom and dad of what they didn't want to hear. Anyway, when we got to Austin, he sold the team and wagon, took us to a store, and told us to buy some good clothes. When me and mother came out of the store, he was in the street with that black horse he bought from you, betting some men he could outrace them. We must have watched them race a dozen times, and he won every race.

"Next he took us to the hotel, and we ate a big supper. But during the meal Daddy didn't say a word. I mean, not one word. Well, when we were finished, he just looked up and said to my mom, 'Honey, I want you and Tashawna to spend the night in this hotel. In the morning you take the stage up to Battle Mountain Station, catch the train to Carson City, and find us a house to rent.'

"He handed us a bag with some money in it. About $300, I think. Mama said she didn't feel comfortable using that stolen money anymore, but Daddy told her this was money he had won in the horse races."

Nathan climbed up on the top rail of the corral fence and looked down at Tashawna.

"So he didn't come with you?"

"No, he said he'd ride that black horse to Carson City, but he wasn't sure when he could get there cause he had to think things through."

"Think things through?"

"I suppose he might be considering giving himself up," she added.

"What makes you suppose that?"

"Well, he looked at me and said, 'Tash, I've got a big job for you. When you get to Galena where they change horses, you go see Nathan and give him this satchel.'"

He jumped down and Tashawna handed him the small leather suitcase.

"What's in it?"

"Almost $20,000."

"The money from the robbery?"

"Yeah."

"But he still robbed the stage . . . I mean, he's got to—"

"Nathan, he's got to figure that out for himself. It's just not as easy for him as it is for you! He said he failed us with the ranch, and he failed us with the hold-up. Nathan, he's not doin' too good, and I'm worried about him. Will you have your dad give this back to the mining company?"

"Sure . . . but you took a chance on coming through here. What if I had you two arrested for, you know, helping him escape?"

She straightened the collar of her coat.

"Daddy said for us not to worry—that 'Nathan will treat you square.' And he's right."

"Tashawna!" Mrs. Cholach called from the stage, "We're ready to leave!"

"Mama's kind of nervous. Will you do it for us, Nathan?"

She reached out and clutched Nathan's arm.

"Yeah, I'll turn it in."

"And . . . eh . . . could you say a little prayer for us sometime? I don't really know when Daddy will join us. If he gets real scared, he just might run to Texas."

"I'll pray," Nathan assured her.

"Listen!" She still held on to one end of the satchel handle as he gripped the other. "Nathan, you come visit us in Carson City. Promise?"

"Eh . . . yeah! I'd like that!" he blustered.

"And please come visit us before you marry that Leah girl."

"Marry? I'm not ever going to marry her. She said she's never going to marry anyone but Kylie Collins."

Crawling up into the stage, Tashawna turned at the door. "Don't you believe her, Nathan Riggins. Don't you ever start believing her."

Suddenly the stage rattled off to the north, and he stood there holding the leather satchel. The case looked new and smelled like a well-oiled saddle. Stepping back over to the side of the corral, he open the little valise and stared at neatly stacked greenbacks.

$20,000! I could buy a ranch, and hundreds of horses, and a new cookstove for mother and . . . No! Some things are just wrong, no matter what!

He closed the satchel and began to walk towards his father's office. He had just passed the bank when Colin Maddison, Jr., (with two d's) came out to the sidewalk and hollered, "Nathan! Guess who I shook hands with at Wells Station!"

"General Sheridan?"

"No. Governor John H. Kinkead!" Colin hurried to keep

Stephen Bly

in step with Nathan. "Anything fun happen while I was gone?"

"Someone robbed the Shiloh stage, and I bought a spotted horse."

"Well, at least one of them's exciting. Hey, what do you have in the bag?"

"It might be full of diamonds and rubies and emeralds!" Nathan teased.

"I don't believe that!"

Nathan continued down the street. "Yeah, well, you wouldn't believe what's in here either!"

"I'm going to go home and eat breakfast. Did you know Miss D'Imperio is back?"

"Great! When does school start up?"

"Tomorrow, I guess."

Colin turned back.

Nathan trudged on down the sidewalk.

Lord, it's going to be pretty rough for Tashawna and her mom if Mr. Cholach never shows up in Carson City. Parents need to be forgiven, too.

He pushed open the door to the marshal's office and saw his father standing by the wood stove reading a telegram.

"Nate, listen to this. Colt Blueman was caught by U.S. Marshal Sandy Thompson near Lewiston in the Idaho Territory. He confessed to robbing a couple of prospectors up at Florence on the day the Shiloh stage was hit. So it couldn't have been Blueman down here. This guy Cholach isn't Blueman, after all. 'Course, I don't suppose that surprises you."

"Nope. But I'll bet you'll be surprised when I show you what's in this leather satchel."

He was.